STAMPEDE AT RATTLESNAKE PASS

When Jake Scudder sees the cloud of dust he knows there's been a stampede. But there is more. A massacre has taken place at Rattlesnake Pass and the Rocking H herd has been rustled, leaving the wrangler Johnnie Parker barely alive. Jake helps the Rocking H owners and escorts Elly Horrocks to Silver City to retrieve the herd. But Jake faces murder, rustlers' bullets and the hangman's noose. Scudder is determined to find those responsible — and make them pay!

CLAY MORE

STAMPEDE AT RATTLESNAKE PASS

Complete and Unabridged

LINFORD
Leicester

First published in Great Britain in 2007 by
Robert Hale Limited
London

First Linford Edition
published 2009
by arrangement with
Robert Hale Limited
London

British Library CIP Data

More, Clay
    Stampede at Rattlesnake Pass.—
    Large print ed.—
    Linford western library
    1. Western stories
    2. Large type books
    I. Title
    823.9'14 [F]

    ISBN 978–1–84782–547–6

Published by
F. A. Thorpe (Publishing)
Anstey, Leicestershire

Set by Words & Graphics Ltd.
Anstey, Leicestershire
Printed and bound in Great Britain by
T. J. International Ltd., Padstow, Cornwall

This book is printed on acid-free paper

For Tricia and Quincy

Prologue

Ben Horrocks struck a light to his cigar as he urged his palomino along the zigzag trail leading down from the mesa. He puffed contentedly for a moment; a man at peace with himself and with his lot in life.

'I love this country, Saul,' he said to the young man riding along beside him. 'It does this old heart of mine good to have you back at the Rocking H. I missed you all that time you was away, boy.'

Ben Horrocks was a tall rangy man with an irongrey moustache and deep wrinkles etched in a darkly tanned face. His son, Saul, was a younger version, clean-shaven, unlined and apparently without a care in the world.

'And I am glad to be back, Pa. When Ma died I figured I just needed some time to cut loose and grow up a bit. But something told me it was time to come home and help you and Elly.' He shook his head and whistled. 'And I reckon whatever told me had got it right. I hadn't realized how hard it must have been for you trying to run the place on your own.'

Ben blew out a ribbon of smoke and squinted up at the blazing midday sun hanging in a cobalt cloudless sky. 'Yes, it has been tough, Saul. But I have a good feeling that we'll be able to turn everything around now.' He patted the bulging saddlebag in front of him. 'With this loan from the Tucksville Bank we will be able to pay the boys what I owe and buy a new bull. I think our luck is about to change, son.'

They reached the bottom of the zigzag and the trail narrowed as it crossed the semi-desert with its numerous saguaro cactus and thickets of yellow-blossomed paloverde.

'I think you're right there, Pa,' Saul replied with a grin. 'What say we speed up some and get this money back to show Elly? My little sister could do with some cheering up. She needs a man in my opinion.'

Ben tossed his head back and gave a short snort-like laugh. 'Well she might get one soon as well. It could be helpful, if you catch my drift.'

'You mean Jeb Jackson at the Double J?'

'That's what I'm thinking. He's real keen, you know.'

In reply Saul raised his hat and gave a loud whoop. 'Well Pa,' he said with a mischievous grin, 'I reckon I'd better hurry off home right now and tell Elly just what you've got in store for her.' And with a kick of his heels he urged his roan down the narrow trail.

'Don't you say any such thing, you young varmint!' Ben cried in mock annoyance. 'Anyways, I reckon my palomino will be home long before that piece of crow bait you call a horse.' And with a guffaw of good humour he kicked his heels to set the big palomino after the roan.

The palomino had only just begun to lengthen its stride as he watched Saul streak past a thicket of paloverde. Then he watched in disbelief as he saw the unmistakable shape of a rifle barrel suddenly protrude from the thicket and discharge. He saw the puff of smoke and heard the report of the gun. And as he flicked his eyes ahead, he saw his son's arms go out and his head shoot backwards as if he had received a battering blow to his back. Then Saul tumbled from the saddle to lie unmoving in the sand.

Fear and anger fought for mastery as Ben reined the palomino in and clawed for the Peacemaker at his side. In his young days he had been no slouch with a gun. He cleared leather, his thoughts now being a tumble of self-preservation, desperation to get to his son and a desire for revenge against this murderous bushwhacker.

As if in slow motion he saw the rifle barrel swivel in his direction as he raised his gun, his thumb ratcheting back the hammer.

But the rifle fired twice in rapid succession, both bullets hammering into his chest. He tumbled backwards off the horse.

And as his life ebbed away he cursed himself for not being there for his son. For not being there for his daughter.

'Luck — just changed . . . ' he gasped as his heart beat its last ever beat.

1

Elly Horrocks stood over the two graves on the butte that marked the highest point of the Rocking H ranch. It was a weekly ritual that she had gone through over the past six months, ever since the bushwhacking of her father and elder brother. Yet it never seemed to get any easier. She laid posies of flowers and said her silent prayers as usual, then shed a few lonely tears before letting herself out of the little picket-fenced enclosure.

'Come on, Trixie,' she said to her sorrel cowpony. 'Let's chase the wind.' She mounted up and let the pony have its head for a mile or two before turning and heading back for home and the depressing atmosphere of the ranch house and all the problems that seemed to go with it. But as she rode back her mind conjured up the image of a young man breaking in a colt. She warmed to his sandy-coloured hair and roguish smile, wishing that he could be riding alongside her now.

'Someday soon we'll be able to tell the world, Trixie,' she said to the back of the sorrel's head, grinning to herself as the animal's ears seemed to prick up with interest. 'But first we need to find a way out of this mess.'

And with her mind now on other more mundane matters she rode up to the ranch house and tied Trixie up at the hitching-post with its cast-iron Rocking H sign atop it. She mounted the steps two at a time, unencumbered as she was by skirts and petticoats, preferring to wear men's range clothes, which did little to conceal her attractive curves. At the door she pulled off her hat, ran a hand through her long corn tresses and let herself in.

'We were worried about you, Miss Elly!' came a gravelly voice from an inner doorway.

She started despite herself and spun round to face Yucatan, her brother's friend and former saddle partner, now the Rocking H general factotum. He was tall, broad-shouldered and narrow-hipped, with angular features and dark complexion. His eyes were sharp, his movements quiet and fast, feline almost. Although he professed Mexican ancestry she suspected that through his veins also flowed Apache blood. He stood in front of her in a black shirt buttoned to the neck and trousers tucked into calf-high soft leather boots.

'I was visiting the graves,' she said, disliking the way that he fussed over her since the shootings.

'It is not a good place. There are rattlesnakes about up there.'

A suitable reply was forming in her mind when another voice called through.

'Elly? Is that you back now? God, I've been worried.'

Elly looked up at Yucatan and fancied she spied a knowing look hover across his lips.

'I said we were worried, Miss Elly,' he said.

She nodded silently as she brushed past him to go through the hall to the main room. A young man was sitting in a Bath chair by the large bay window, a paper in one hand and a wad of documents on his blanket-covered knees. His resemblance to her was unmistakable; same corn-coloured hair, blue eyes and lightly dimpled chin. Yet there was a hardness, a bitterness about the mouth that was foreign to Elly's visage. She was aware that it never used to be there on him.

'I've only been visiting Ma and Pa's graves, Saul,' she said, taking in the worried expression.

Saul Horrocks dropped the paper on top of the others, shook his head and smiled past her as Yucatan entered and stood a pace behind her shoulder. 'It would have been three graves up there if my friend Yucatan hadn't found me.'

'We are friends, Master Saul. You saved my life once, now I will always look after you.'

Elly felt her cheeks redden as a surge

of guilt came to consciousness. She knew that it had been such a close thing. If Yucatan hadn't found them that morning then her brother would have bled to death with a bullet in his spine. There had been nothing that he could do for her father, of course. And the murderers, whoever they were, had stolen the money they had just borrowed from the bank. As it was, Yucatan had taken her father and brother back in the buckboard and while the hands took care of Ben Horrocks's body, in the absence of a trained medical man Yucatan had removed the bullet himself with a red-hot knife, then cauterized the wound. Undoubtedly, it had saved his life, but apparently the bullet had smashed his spine and permanently taken away the use of his legs. Over the months that followed Yucatan had looked after all of Saul's manly needs, while Elly saw to feeding him back to some semblance of health.

'I should be dead, Elly!'

She dropped down on one knee beside him and took his right hand. 'Well, you are not dead, Saul, so don't get maudlin again. Please! You have still got me, and I am here for you, Saul.'

Suddenly, anger flared, as it seemed to do so often these days. He viciously raised a fist and brought it down on his thigh, scattering the papers on the floor. 'Goddammit! There's no feeling there, Elly, I might just as well be dead for all the use that I am. I am condemned to this chair and I can't run a ranch from here, can I?'

'We will manage, Saul,' she protested.

His eyes flashed upwards, challengingly. 'How, Elly?' he queried, a tone of desperation having crept into his voice. He pointed to the papers on the floor. Yucatan crossed the room and silently began picking the sheaves up. He stacked them into a pile which he laid on the nearby table.

'Bills, bills! How are we going to pay them off?' Saul went on. 'We're getting deeper in debt every day — and now the bank are threatening to foreclose on us.' He gritted his teeth and thumped his other thigh with his other fist. 'That damned bank knows that those dirty bushwhackers stole the money Pa borrowed, but Wilber Goodson, the new manager, had that letter delivered to me today. They won't wait more than another two weeks.'

Elly gasped. She straightened and walked to the window, looking out at some of the ranch hands going about their early-morning chores. Her eyes fell on one in particular, leading a couple of horses towards the corral, and for a moment her anxiety was distracted.

She heard Saul sigh, then:

'Elly, there is still one way — '

She spun round, her mouth firm. 'No, Saul! We've been through all this before. I will not marry Jeb Jackson.'

Saul nodded to the tall Yucatan. 'Give us a moment, will you? I could do with some coffee.'

With a nod the factotum left silently.

'Now see here, Elly, the morning we were — shot — Pa told me that — '

'I won't consider it, Saul. Jeb Jackson is near twice my age and I — I don't love him. I can't! I won't do it!'

Saul clicked his tongue. 'Then we only have a couple of weeks to find enough money to pay back the loan and stop the bank foreclosing. We've got to show them that we have plans — big plans! But first we need to raise money.'

'How, Saul? What can we sell?'

He hesitated for a moment. 'I hoped it wouldn't come to this, but I have been thinking. We sell half the herd, straight away. Then we pay the bank and instead of buying a bull like Pa planned, we buy sheep. We'll have to tighten our belts, cut back on some of the luxuries, but with a good price for our beeves at Silver City and a whole parcel of luck we might manage it. I reckon we can sell half the herd at Silver City, then go south and buy a goodly sized flock of Navaho-Churro sheep, then we can start to build the biggest sheep ranch in the territory. Meat and fleece, we might just manage it.'

Elly looked at her brother in amazement. 'Sheep? You want us to become sheep-farmers? Pa would turn — ' She bit her lip as she realized what she had said. 'I mean, we've always been cattle-ranchers.'

'Then maybe it's time to change, Elly. The way I see it, we can breed sheep for meat and wool and keep half the range for the beef.' He held his hands palm upwards. 'We have to do something real different if we are to survive all this.'

Elly puffed her cheeks. 'I guess so. I just never thought of anything as different as that. But you are talking about a drive, now? Surely we don't have enough men to drive half the herd? That would be two thousand head.'

'We'll hire more men.' He flashed her a smile of encouragement which, for a moment, seemed to have the humour that she remembered him having in abundance before the shooting. 'What say you go and get Bill Coburn and whichever of the boys he can bring in and I'll feed them the deal.' Again the smile played across his lips, then:

'Go on, little El,' he said with a wink, using his old term of affection for her. 'Yucatan will have the coffee rustled up by the time you get back.'

★ ★ ★

Bill Coburn had been Ben Horrocks's ramrod for nigh on twenty years and knew just about everything there was to know about ranching. He was a bow-legged old puncher with thinning hair and a posture that looked as if he could be poured into a saddle. He sat uneasily on the leather settee on the opposite side of the bay window from Saul. Beside him, looking equally uneasy, as if he feared dirtying the seating, sat Johnnie Parker, the Rocking H wrangler, a sandy-haired,

16

good-looking young man of about twenty years.

If both men seemed slightly uneasy it was for different reasons. Bill never felt sure how to talk to his employer, Saul Horrocks, and had to admit to a slight prejudice about his having taken off for a couple of years after his mother Elizabeth Horrocks had died from a fever. He sympathized with him all right for having lost his pa and getting shot up, but he somehow doubted that he had the ability to make the ranch work. As for Johnnie, his unease was caused by the fact that Elly Horrocks was standing pouring coffee for them and he was studiously trying not to look at her. When she eventually handed him a cup and saucer it was all he could do to not let it rattle too much.

Elly smiled to herself, then sat on the chair beside her father's old roll-top desk. Yucatan stood by the door, arms folded in front of him.

Saul Horrocks was frank. He laid his cards before them as to the precarious situation that the ranch was in.

'So you see, boys, we have no choice. We have to diversify and start building a name for sheep in these parts.' He hesitated a moment, then asked: 'Unless either of you can think of some other way out of this mess?'

Bill placed his cup and saucer on the floor by his feet. 'Sheep?' he repeated in disbelief. 'I never thought I would end up chasing sheep.' He gave a shrug of resignation. 'But if that's what we have to do, then so be it. So first you need us to move half the herd to Silver City? That'll be a tall order with just five men.'

'Then hire another three or four. They'll get paid at Silver City.'

'It'll take at least a couple of days to get ready.'

'That's all the time you've got. The bank will foreclose in two weeks. Silver City is about sixty miles from here, so it'll take several days if you push them hard. Coming back will be quicker, of course.'

Bill sighed and rose to his feet. 'Reckon I had better get onto it right away then.' He tapped Johnnie on the shoulder. 'Come on boy, you go tell the others what's happening while I head into Tucksville and try to do some hiring. The way I see it, we've got to make this work or we're all out on our ears.'

Johnnie saw Elly start to gather cups and saucers. He swiftly scooped up Bill's cup and saucer from the floor and carried them over to the table. 'Let me take that tray, Miss Elly.'

She thanked him and led the way past Yucatan to the kitchen. Once there Johnnie deposited the tray on the table, then turned as she willingly fell into his arms and they kissed passionately.

'We need to tell your brother, Elly,' he whispered as they parted.

'I know, but not yet. Not when we face losing the Rocking H.' She brushed invisible dust from his sleeve. 'You help Bill get that herd sold, then we'll see.'

Johnnie's face creased into that

roguish smile she loved so much. 'Elly, if it means we can be together I reckon I can become the best damned shepherd since Joseph himself in the good book.'

★ ★ ★

Jeb Jackson was a proud man. A rich man who had built up the Double J spread through hard endeavour and business savvy, with a streak of ruthlessness tempered by a measure of fair play. Now in his prime, at least in his own estimation, he wanted someone to share the fruits of his toil and success; someone who could give him companionship and more — help him establish a dynasty to pass his wealth to.

And he had set his sights on Elly Horrocks — if she would have him.

'Damn it, Jeb!' he exclaimed to himself as he stood looking at the full-length mirror in the dressing-room adjoining his bedroom, struggling to tie one of the fancy French bow ties that he had had sent from New Orleans. 'You are all fingers and thumbs — and you've made a fine hash of it.'

With a curse he pulled it off and yanked open a drawer, from which he drew out a fresh bandanna instead. He knotted it about his neck, immediately feeling more comfortable. 'What do you think you are playing at? Dressing up like some city slicker to try and impress the girl?'

He swivelled right and left to assess his reflection. In truth, he had to admit that he was not displeased with himself. Hard work and being careful with his vices had enabled him to keep a trim enough figure, and he had been fortunate to have kept his hair, in both quantity and colour. He ran a finger across his equally dark moustache, then picked up his Stetson and made for the door.

He thought of what he was going to say as he rode alone along the trail towards the Rocking H.

Poor old Ben Horrocks, he thought.

21

He never had much luck, poor guy. And his son Saul; how happy Ben had been when his prodigal son came home — only for Ben to get shot through the heart and Saul to get backshot and crippled. Effectively it had left Elly Horrocks, the best-looking girl this side of the Pintos, more or less alone to run the ranch while her brother was nursed back to health by that Mexican friend of his, Yucatan.

'I'm going to try and change all that,' he mused to himself. Then with a grin: 'I'll take her away from all that care.'

But as he rode up the main Rocking H trail towards the ranch-house he noticed that there seemed to be something odd about the place. There were men going about their business, but he surely didn't recognize them all. He knew virtually all of the cowhands in the area, but a couple of these were *vaqueros* from south of the border. A voice inside his head told him that preparations were being made for a trail drive. It was an impression confirmed by Cookie O'Toole, the grizzled old Rocking H commissary, who had once worked on a drive for Jeb. He was busily stocking up a chuck wagon with barrels, cooking utensils and supplies of sourdough, pork-belly, beans and bags of coffee.

'Odd time to be mounting a drive, Cookie,' he commented as he drew to a halt by the wagon.

'Needs must, I reckon,' replied Cookie, removing a worn old Confederate cap and wiping his brow with the back of a hamlike forearm. 'Boss man says we have to start chasing sheep instead of critters if we want to stave the bank thieves off.' He turned his head and spat contemptuously in the dust.

Jeb dismounted and produced a couple of cigars from his vest. He proffered one to Cookie and clipped the other between his lips. 'Sheep in this area? That may not be popular with some of Saul's neighbouring ranchers. Tell me more.'

Over their cigars the old commissary told as much as he knew, ever since the day of the bush-whacking which had so shocked and horrified the territory. He told him all that he himself had been told by Bill Coburn and Johnnie Parker without any feeling of disloyalty, for his past dealings with Jeb Jackson had always shown him to be a straight-shooter, a man you could trust.

At last Jeb took a final puff on his cigar and ground the butt out under the heel of an expensive boot. 'I sure wish you luck, Cookie. Reckon I best go and have a chat with Saul. Maybe I could help out as one neighbour to another.'

A few moments later, as he tied up to the hitching-post, then mounted the steps to the main door of the ranch house Jeb Jackson allowed himself a half-smile.

So they were finding it all a bit difficult? That was good, he thought. At least it would be a good time to put forward any proposition he might have.

He tapped on the door and waited

for the sound of feet crossing the hall towards the door. As he saw the door handle move he cursed himself for not having had the foresight to bring flowers. His mouth creased into a smile as the door opened and he felt his heart speed up at the sight of the woman he wanted to be his wife. Then it skipped a beat when she smiled back — a polite smile, but without any warmth. He knew it was going to be hard.

2

Johnnie Parker had been blessed with high good humour, which was just as well, he thought, considering that he was riding drag to a 2,000-head drive. He grinned to himself behind his bandanna, which was pulled up over his face leaving only a narrow slit between it and his turned-down Stetson for him to see out of.

'Liars, the whole danged lot of them,' he announced to the back of the bay's head. 'If I had my way I would take every one of those darned Eastern dime novelists and make them walk behind a herd like this, instead of spreading lies about the romance of riding the range. All you get is dust, dry eyes and wagonloads of dung.'

And as he thought about how thirsty he was his mind jumped ahead with joyous anticipation to the delight of savouring the first mug of Arbuckle's coffee that Cookie would have ready for them when they eventually bedded the herd down for the night. It was after mid-afternoon and as usual at this time Cookie had gone on ahead of the herd to find a suitable spot to have their meal ready when bed-down time came.

They were on the third day out from the ranch and had made a steady fifteen miles a day along the trail. Good open land it was too, so that the long procession could be coaxed along without feeling too nervous, which was always a potential problem when there were a few frolicsome steers in the bunch.

'We've gone well, feller,' Johnnie informed the bay. 'We should get to Silver City tomorrow, then you and me is going to wet our whistles real well. You with some of that sweet Silver City water, and me with a bucket of cold beer from the Busted Flush saloon.' He chuckled behind his bandanna. 'And Cookie will probably sit himself in some corner with that chimney-stack pipe of his and drink a couple of glasses of milk, like he always does. The old fool thinks we all believe that he doesn't drink hard liquor, but we've all seen him lace his milk and his coffee with good red-eye tonsil paint.'

He turned his attention to the undulating drag end of the herd, to where all the footsore steers, the infants and the lazy critters gravitated. He kicked his heels and urged the bay towards a couple of stragglers, coaxing them to speed up with a couple of flicks of his rope.

'What do you think of that Bill Coburn, eh feller? Telling me that I had promotion from wrangler to drag rider.' He turned and waved to the young Mexican *vaquero* who was trailing about a couple of hundred yards back with the remuda. 'Hey Emilio, keep up there or you'll miss out on supper.'

The young Mexican waved back, although Johnnie doubted whether he had actually heard him. He turned his attention back to the herd that loomed ahead of him half-hidden in the cloud of sand and dust that 8,000 hoofs were kicking up. Screwing his eyes up he could dimly see the two flank riders about a third of the way up the herd, one on each side, and another third of the way he made out the two swing men. All of them were moving up and down the sides, blocking critters from cutting loose or just meandering away from the main body.

'Old Bill did well to hire these fellers,' Johnnie informed his bay. 'They all seem to know their stuff and there is no way we could have managed with just the five Rocking H crew. Two of them don't have much sense of humour, but hell — neither does Cookie.'

In the far distance, at the head of the herd, he could just make out Bill Coburn's characteristic riding posture as he and Skeeter Carson rode point on each shoulder of the herd. He watched as Bill moved inwards, simultaneously signalling for Skeeter to move outwards to begin turning the herd to the right in the direction of the Pintos foothills.

'Looks like we're heading towards Rattlesnake Pass, feller,' he informed his uninterested bay. 'It's a dismal rocky place that I can't say I cotton to. Especially if there really are rattlers around there. Last thing we want is for some motherly rattler to spook some of these critters.' And with a shiver he turned his mind to more attractive thoughts.

The mental image of Elly Horrocks appeared in his mind, just as she had been a few days before, naked and beautiful as ever as they made love in her big brass bed. And she had certainly been passionate, almost violent in her love-making, like a wild animal. Then afterwards, as they lay spent together, she had confessed that she had been angry.

'It was that man Jeb Jackson. He had the audacity to come calling on us — on Saul — to ask him to put in a good word with me.' Johnnie grinned as he recalled her pretty face flush with pique. 'He . . . he's so old! Oh Johnnie, we need to get away together!' she exclaimed.

'Soon, Elly,' he mused to the horse's head in front of him, as he pulled his bandanna up even further to protect his face. 'Soon I'll be back and we can start making plans.'

★   ★   ★

Bill Coburn was worried; a natural enough state of mind for any trail boss. After all, he had a heavy burden of responsibility on his shoulders. If the Rocking H ranch was to survive he had to get the best price he could at Silver City and get back to the ranch pronto. And until they got there he had the responsibility for 2,000 head of beeves and eight men, all of which necessitated that he be here, there and everywhere.

'Good man, that Skeeter,' he mused to himself once they had successfully turned the herd in the direction of Rattlesnake Pass.

He signalled to Skeeter over the heads of the herd using the prearranged set of hand signals that they had agreed upon to indicate that he was going to ride on ahead to meet up with Cookie. But before he actually did so he wheeled his big stallion round and repeated the hand-signals to Curlie Shanks, the swing rider on the same side of the herd, so that he could ride up the string to cover Bill's point position.

'Hope the old fool hasn't gone too far,' he said to himself as he set off at a gentle trot so as not to spook any potentially nervous critters at the front.

Once he had put some distance between himself and the head of the herd he let the stallion have its head as he made his way through the pass that threaded its way through the Pintos. It was a sheer walled, U-shaped canyon renowned, possibly more in legend than in fact, for its regular population of rattlesnakes. Countless trails led off it into a maze of canyons.

At the thought of the name Bill guffawed. 'The whole blamed territory has its god-given share of rattlers, right enough — but a man could live his life here without seeing any, on account of them liking human company less than we like them and their tell-tale noise.'

The ruts of the chuck wagon showed clearly in the semi-desert floor of the canyon, confirming that Cookie had passed through all right.

'Which just goes to show that a hot chuck wagon driven by a whiskey-sodden commissary makes a whole lot better time than a parcel of critters driven by eight sober men,' he joked to himself.

Then, as he negotiated the U-bend of the pass, he saw the chuck wagon some distance ahead, already unhitched on a slight rise.

'Cookie, you sensible old buzzard,' he said aloud. 'There isn't any sense in pitching camp on ground where the herd is going to bed down. Looks like you haven't had too much rot-gut yet, anyhow.'

And he noticed the ribbon of smoke rising from the fire that Cookie had already started in preparation for the evening meal. He prodded his horse's flanks with his heels and rode to within about fifty yards before he slowed down to a trot.

As he approached he noticed the extra horse beyond the chuck wagon, then he saw that the old commissary was not alone. A muscle twitched in his back and he tensed involuntarily as he recognized the gruff tone that belonged to a puncher who had worked for the Rocking H until Ben Horrocks had fired him the previous year, on his recommendation.

'Well, lookie here — it's the boss man, Bill Coburn,' came the voice. 'Come for some of your coffee, I expect, Cookie.'

'What are you doing here, Fleming?' Bill queried suspiciously.

Hog Fleming was a fat-cheeked man with a slightly porcine air about him. He smiled obsequiously as he swirled coffee in a tin mug. 'Hey, what's up, Bill? You don't sound too friendly to a former Rocking H man.' Then the smile faded completely. 'But then you never were very friendly, were you. Got me fired for no good reason, didn't you.'

'I asked what you are doing here?' Bill repeated. 'I didn't like you being around the Rocking H and I sure don't like seeing you here on my trail drive.'

'Free country, Bill. I just happened to meet up with my old friend Cookie here and he offered me a coffee.'

'No coffee for you, Fleming. This may be a free country but as far as you are concerned this chuck wagon is Rocking H property and you are not welcome. Now git!'

Hog Fleming looked down at the tin coffee-mug in his hand. 'Now that is plumb bad-mannered, Coburn. I can't abide bad manners.'

Cookie had been standing with a

coffee-mug of his own in his hand and his chimney pipe in his mouth. He pulled the pipe out and tapped Hog Fleming on the shoulder. 'Easy there, Hog. Bill here is the boss and you had better — '

He never finished. There was the explosion of a gunshot and Cookie staggered backwards. He looked down in disbelief at the spreading patch of crimson on the front of his vest.

'Hog, what the . . . ?' He slowly fell forward into the dust.

Bill Coburn had watched him fall with a look of shock and disbelief. Then realization dawned upon him as he saw the smoking gun in Hog Fleming's hand. A desire for retribution coupled with an instinct for sheer self-preservation sent his hand flying towards his own gun. For a working ranch foreman he had a relatively fast draw, but desperation made him faster. He cleared leather faster than he had ever done before — only to realize that even that had not been fast enough.

He felt a thud in his belly, immediately followed by a feeling of intense heat, as if he had been skewered by a red-hot poker. And in that instant he knew that he was a dead man.

Despite the agony he managed to raise his gun in the direction of his killer and even managed to draw back the hammer, intent on taking the bastard with him.

But another bullet smashed into his brain, killing him instantly and robbing him of the satisfaction of knowing that as his body convulsed, his hand had squeezed the trigger and blown off the lobe of Hog Fleming's left ear.

★　★　★

Rubal Cage liked to dress in black, because he felt it suited his moods and the image that he wanted to project. Men were wary of black-haired *hombres* in black rig, he believed. He felt it gave them a sense that he was a man who could deal out death. Indeed, he was a man full of hate. It wasn't so much that life had dealt him a bad hand of cards, more the fact that he was more sensitive and had a longer memory than most folks. Any slight against him was stored up and locked away until he saw a way of getting even. Minor slights merited a beating of some sort and major ones usually deserved death, in his view.

Having been fired from the Double J ranch was definitely a major slight in his mind. He was nurturing the hate he felt towards the rancher, using it even to generate the emotion he needed to carry out his work.

'Your time will come soon enough, you bastard!' he cursed as he pictured how the rancher would meet his maker — before his time. And with murder in his heart he stroked the butt-plate of his Winchester .73 and signalled to the others to start closing in on the herd up ahead.

'Yes sir, until then we'll have a little practice!' he said to himself, his mouth drawing into a thin cruel curve.

* ★ ★ ★

Emilio Sanchez's mind was not on his job. Looking after the string of highly strung cowponies was not his idea of what a *vaquero* was all about. Even to ride drag would have suited him, but he was aware that beggars could not be choosers. And ever since his father had died and Emilio had been forced to fend for his mother and his nine sisters there had been times when begging was not far off. Although he was hardly able to ride, he had been grateful to Ramirez for lying to the gringo ramrod about him being an experienced *vaquero*, which was his actual ambition.

As usual when times were hard, Emilio retreated into the land of make-believe. Instead of a humble wrangler he had a picture of himself as a dangerous desperado masquerading as a wrangler in order to gain the trust of a wealthy rancher, so that he could make the lovely daughter fall in love with him, just like in the dime novels

39

that he so loved to read.

So distracted was he with his own posturing as he played the part in his own imagined dime novel that he did not hear the soft approach of a rider behind him. When he did hear, he turned in the saddle, his usual friendly smile flashing across his youthful visage.

It was wiped away the instant that he felt a thud in his chest and felt the searing agony of the blade, tossed from a distance of twenty feet, as it punctured his ribcage and found his heart.

'No *señor!*' he gasped, staring at this nameless killer. 'I have a mother! I have sisters. I am . . . '

His pony trotted after the retreating herd as Emilio Sanchez slid from the saddle to fall dead in the sand.

★   ★   ★

Rubal Cage had chosen his men well. All of them had killed before, without hesitation and without any lasting impression on their consciences. Men after his own heart, which of course made them extra dangerous because they would undoubtedly betray their own mother — or even worse — betray him, if the price or the need was right. Yet while they saw the advantage in it they were all happy to follow his orders to the letter — as they had done in surreptitiously surrounding the herd and the riders driving it.

He himself had taken out the wrangler kid while they had scattered to easily outflank the herd and cowboys by using the stacks and natural cover provided by saguaro and scrub-oak thickets to conceal their advance. Thus far it had all gone to plan, the aim being to get into position before the herd turned into Rattlesnake Pass.

Rubal Cage recognized the drag rider by the way he sat his horse as well as by the clothes he wore. He recognized him because he was already aware that he had a special relationship with the Horrocks girl, who he himself had designs on. It was for that reason that he didn't simply back shoot the kid, but rode to within hailing distance above the noise of the advancing herd.

'Put your hands up and turn around, real slow, cowboy!' he barked out.

Johnnie Parker stiffened in the saddle when he heard the words. Shrewd enough to realize that death was possible if he acted otherwise, he turned his head slowly, his hands raised above his head.

'That you, Cage?' he queried, squinting above the bandanna that was still above his nose. 'What the hell are you doing here — with a gun?'

'Come visiting, what you think?' replied Rubal Cage. 'Wanted to pass on my respects to the dead.'

Johnnie screwed his eyes even more. 'The dead? Who's dead?'

'You!' snapped Rubal Cage. 'I just wanted you to know that your girl will be taken care of.'

Johnnie's eyes blazed and he went for his gun. But just as Bill Coburn had failed to draw fast enough, so Johnnie was no match for a man with his gun already drawn and aimed. Rubal Cage's gun spat two bullets in rapid succession, each scoring a hit on Johnnie's chest, so powerful that he was thrown backwards to fall over the horse's rump into the sand.

'I'll take care of her real well,' said Cage as he holstered his sidearm and rode past the prostrate body. 'I promise.'

In the distance he fancied that he heard a succession of shots from different locations about the herd.

Then there was a deafening cacophony of bellowing and moaning from the herd. Rubal Cage pulled out his Winchester .73 from its scabbard and let off several shots above the heads of the rear-most critters. He grinned as an undulating motion began, gaining momentum until the whole herd was racing forward. The herd of 2,000 head rushed headlong towards Rattlesnake Pass.

3

The sudden noise of thunder, totally unexpected in the heat of a late afternoon beneath a cloudless, cobalt-blue sky roused Jake Scudder from the daydream he had been indulging in as he ambled across the semi-desert towards the Pintos. Then about five or six miles ahead he saw the slow rise of a long, low dust cloud. Instantly he realized that he was watching the start of a cattle stampede.

He frowned when along with the thunderous clamour he heard distant cracking noises. He reckoned that some of the riders were probably trying to bring down some of the leaders to halt the stampeding herd's progress. He well knew that running alongside a stampeding herd was no place that a sane man would want to be, yet it was just part of the job that a puncher signed up for.

As he watched the progress of the dust cloud and listened with cocked ears to the accompanying thunder he realized that the herd was heading towards the Pintos Mountains. That meant that the cattle trail presumably followed in the direction of some pass that he could not discern from his distance and the angle that he was approaching from.

Scudder sighed and tossed up in his mind whether or not he should investigate. He pulled off his Stetson and ran his fingers through his thick black hair, freeing a goodly cloud of trail dust as he did so. He was a tall, handsome fellow with a three-day growth of stubble, which mirrored the fatigue he felt after his long ride from Sonora via Tucksville. His clothes were covered in a patina of south-western desert sand and dirt, his throat was parched and the back of his neck burned from an overdose of Arizonan sun on his exposed skin.

'Not really any of my business, is it, old horse?' he remarked to his big black stallion. Then after a moment he guffawed as he gave in at last to his conscience. He couldn't in his heart ignore the plight that some riders might find themselves in over there. A stampede almost always resulted in casualties, both to critters and to humans. 'Guess we'd better pay a visit and see if we can be of any service. They might need me, my rope and you, you big heap of horseflesh.'

The stallion tossed its head and snickered, as if it well understood both his words and his sense of humour. And a few moments later they were picking their way towards the fast retreating stampede and its accompanying dust cloud.

*　*　*

One thing that Rubal Cage prided himself upon was his knowledge of critters. He somehow understood the way they thought, both as individual ornery beasts and when they were moving together as a herd. He had worked with them for all of his adult life — on both sides of the law — as a regular puncher and ramrod, and as a brand-buster, in between spells as a road agent or hired gun. And he knew just how to work them either way. Yet the thing that he was proudest of was his knowledge of the way a herd worked when it was stampeding, when it was running flat out without direction. He knew, probably better than most, on account of the fact that he had orchestrated stampedes on numerous occasions in the past.

And nowhere offered a better place to stampede and control a herd than the Rattlesnake Pass in the Pintos. The natural lie of the land and the way the pass turned about on itself in a natural U-shape meant that the cattle naturally slowed down as they navigated the bend.

'And that's just where you'll be

waiting for them,' he had told Hog Fleming and Cole Lancing before they had set off at the beginning of the venture. 'Hog, I reckon that you'll have to deal with the cook first, because they're bound to send him through the pass first to get chow ready for when they bed the herd down. Then the two of you find a place up in the rocks and be ready for when we stampede the herd. They'll be coming round that U-bend as though Old Nick is chasing their tails, and that's when I want you to shoot the lead steers on the far side. That'll start the herd to turn and once they get into that part of the pass that opens out they'll begin to circle on themselves. There is just enough room for them to begin that circle, and if you take down a few more, they'll soon slow up and then they'll stop.'

And indeed, that was exactly what happened as the stampede hurtled round the bend. Fleming and Lancing were waiting up in the canyon wall and they took down about ten lead steers, then a few more as the herd started to circle on itself. The dust cloud was as thick as smoke, but it eventually settled on the gasping herd and the rustlers.

'Goddamit!' Rubal Cage exclaimed joyfully as he rode up with the other rustlers to meet Hog Fleming and Cole Lancing. 'That was the slickest job I ever did see.' He noticed the blood-soaked bandanna wrapped around Hog Fleming's ear. 'What the hell happened to you? Did that cook give you some trouble?'

Fleming scowled. 'No! Him I dealt with easily. And that blasted ramrod, Coburn.' He spat contemptuously on the ground. 'As Coburn was dying his gun went off and a stray shot — '

Rubal Cage guffawed. 'A stray shot creased your ear? An inch inwards and it would have creased your brain, and then you would have been herding cattle in a hotter hell-hole than here.'

Lancing, a coarse-featured young man with a lazy eye sneered at his companion's discomfiture. 'But what about the bodies, Rubal? Are we just going to leave them there on the trail?'

Cage shook his head. 'You know that gully we passed as you went aways into Rattlesnake Pass? I reckon that would make a good place to bury the witnesses. We'll just leave the beef carcases where they are, though. The buzzards will soon strip them clean.'

*   *   *

The stallion was a powerful beast and would have galloped all the way if Jake Scudder had allowed it. But he was all too aware that the black's strength would be needed, as likely as not, once they reached the eventual resting place of the herd — once it had run out of pace and the front critters either collapsed from exhaustion or were themselves run down. And all of that could add miles to the journey. So he held the stallion in check a mite, content to simply catch up as best they could, so that they could be of some use at the end of the chase.

As he glanced upwards, the appearance from nowhere of a brace of buzzards was not unexpected. 'You devils always seem to know when there is a good dinner of fresh flesh, don't you,' he said jocularly. 'There's bound to be a few dead critters and a few that are too crippled to walk.'

He cringed at the idea of all the creatures that would play their part in stripping the flesh from the bones, from the buzzards and coyotes to the maggots that would finish the job to leave bare bones for the sun and sand to bleach. Then the skeletons would decorate the desert with more ornaments of death.

Jake Scudder was ever a humorous man, yet the buzzards' appearance unsettled him more than he would have expected.

'I have a bad feeling about them, old horse,' he confided to the black as they approached the Pintos and he saw the entrance to a pass opening before them. The ground was all churned up from the stampeding herd.

'I reckon this must be the famous Rattlesnake Pass we heard about back in Tucksville when we passed through. I guess any rattlers that lived here would have skedaddled out of the way once they felt the vibration of that coming stampede.' He chuckled. 'But let's you and me just step careful in case any come out to look after the procession that just passed through. They might be a touch angry.' And at the thought he winced, for snakes were not Jake Scudder's favourite creatures.

Entering Rattlesnake Pass was an eye-opener for Scudder. It was huge; great sheer red rock walls with occasional patches of green as various cacti and shrubbery had seeded themselves in cracks and crevices to gain a precarious yet sustainable foothold on life. The air was stuffy, thick with settling dust and sand, so he slowed down to take a drink from his canteen to wash the dust from his throat. He had just put the stopper back in the canteen and pulled up his bandanna over his nose when he heard the unmistakeable reports of gunfire, each shot followed by a cacophony of echoes from all around Rattlesnake Pass.

'Sounds as if there's a puncher at work, putting a few crippled or dying critters out of their misery,' he said conversationally to the back of the black's head.

The horse flared its nostrils and stamped a forefoot, a gesture that he recognized as an indication that the horse was displeased with something.

'You don't like that idea, do you, old feller?' Jake asked, shaking his head. 'And neither do I, but I also hate to see any creature suffering. Come on, let's see if we can help whoever is up ahead. It sounds as if he's someways around that bend ahead.'

As he let the black trot its way along the pass he heard several more shots followed by another series of echoes bouncing off the canyon walls. As he turned the great U-bend of the pass, in the distance he saw the source of the gunfire. A lone rider was sitting astride a palomino aiming a rifle down into a hollow.

'Some of the poor critters must have gone dashing down a ravine or gully,' he mused to the black. He raised his hand to his mouth, positioning his thumb and forefinger against his tongue to produce a loud, high-pitched whistle, at which those who were practised in the ways of cow-punching were usually adept. It rang out along the pass, producing its own rippling echo effect.

The effect on the shooter was instantaneous — and unexpected!

He turned in his saddle, spied Jake and immediately trained his rifle at him, letting off a couple of quick shots. Both were too close for comfort, one actually lifting his hat from his head and depositing it on the ground behind him.

'Hey!' Jake cried, but a third shot ricocheted off the canyon wall and he felt a shower of grit from the point of impact on the rock. Further remonstration or question was clearly futile. What was demanded was cover and a little return fire.

Jake's mind raced as he considered his options. Turning to retreat was not an option, since he would expose his back as a target to someone who just about had his range. Similarly, a headlong charge would expose him to greater risk as he closed the gap, and a stationary shooter had an infinitely greater chance of success than a galloping rider trying to shoot. He was only left with a half-way approach.

So he spurred the black forward, leaning low in the saddle and drawing his own Winchester from its boot. Two more bullets zinged overhead; he raised his rifle and let off two quick shots himself, albeit with little hope of accuracy. Yet the other's reaction told him that one of his shots had an effect. The man clamped a hand to his ear as a red rag or something fell from the side of his head. Then, as if stung into rage he lifted his rifle again. Scudder, seeing the man taking longer to aim whispered to the black: 'You are on your own for a while, old feller. I'm gonna leave you now.'

And so saying, when he heard the next report he threw his hands upwards and flung himself from the saddle to land behind a tangle of scrub-oak. The instant he hit the ground he rolled over three times in order to change his position lest the gunman had pin-pointed where he had fallen. Gingerly, he slid the barrel of his Winchester through an opening and squinted through the gap to see if his ruse had worked. He figured that if he played possum then the guy would either come in for the kill or, less likely, he would take off.

To Jake's surprise he did the latter. As he spurred the palomino into action he saw the rider head off with one hand clamped to his left ear. Moments later all he heard was the fast retreating cadence of galloping hoofs going round the bend of the pass.

'Now just what the hell was that all about?' he asked himself as he came to his feet, brushing the fresh accumulation of sand and dirt that he had picked up in his tumble.

He whistled and the big stallion came trotting over to him. Jake sheathed his Winchester and climbed into the saddle. 'I best see what the bastard didn't want me to see,' he said aloud, his eye catching sight again of the circling buzzards high overhead.

The sight that greeted him a few moments later, as he dismounted and stood atop the gulley made him feel sick to his stomach. There were the bodies of nine men piled on top of one another, as if they had been casually tossed down into the gully.

Jake's stomach went into spasm and he tasted bile in the back of his throat. Every one of the men had several bullet wounds and they had bled copiously.

'A massacre! What sort of curs would do something like this?' And seeing that a couple of them were little more than boys, he felt a surge of fury. Then he shook his head at the sadness of it all. 'The poor devils. And that's what the bastard was doing. Making sure that no one survived.' Then the fury was replaced in part by a feeling of guilt. 'Maybe if I had been here faster, I might have been able to save some of them.'

The shadows of the circling scavengers reminded him that he needed to act quickly. After all, it was not just the buzzards that he had to think about, it was the possibility that the gunman might return with reinforcements.

'Reckon I had better try and cover you gents up to protect your bodies from those varmints,' he said. 'Leastways until I get help from Tucksville and get you taken care of properly.'

As he gingerly made his way down to see what he could do, he was surprised to hear a low moan. One of them was still alive.

★   ★   ★

Jake worked as quickly as he could. Having located the young man who seemed to be precariously clinging to life, and having checked to ensure that there were no other survivors, he extricated him from between two bodies. 'these comrades of yours seem to have saved your life, my friend.' Then hoisting him on one shoulder he carried him up to the top of the hollow.

He found a shady spot below a great boulder and had a good look at the two upper-body wounds that the young man had sustained. Fortunately, neither bullet wound had hit a major vessel, and as far as he could tell from listening to the young man's chest, neither one had penetrated a lung. One had gouged a groove through muscle on the side of the chest and the other had seemingly smashed a collarbone and somehow been deflected upwards and outwards, exiting at the top of his shoulder at the back, presumably missing the top of his lung. Jake washed the wounds and stanched the flow of blood as best he could by shredding one of his shirts from his saddle-bag and using it as padding and crude bandaging.

'Can't say that you were lucky, mister', he said to the still unconscious young man as he moistened his lips from the canteen. 'The only thing is that you weren't as unlucky as your poor friends down there.'

With a sigh and a final look up at the buzzards he made his way down to the bottom of the gulley and laid the bodies out as respectfully as he could, before covering them with scrub-oak, rocks and sand. He hoped that it would not be too long before they would be taken back to Tucksville, or wherever they were from, and have a proper burial with their families present. Anything would be better than this ignominious gully in Rattlesnake Pass, he concluded.

It was as he was gently lifting the young man into the saddle that he noticed the bloodstained bandanna that the murderer had dropped. He lifted it and examined it, noticing the bullet hole, presumably from his own bullet. 'So somebody had hit you, too,' he said with a feeling of satisfaction. 'Well I reckon that you'll have a couple of tell-tale wounds on you — you murdering dog!'

★   ★   ★

The going was not easy, trying to avoid too much jostling to the injured man. Every couple of hours Scudder stopped to let both the unconscious patient and the stallion rest. It was during one of these stops beside a small spring that the patient stirred, his eyes flickering open.

'Elly — got to see — Elly!'

Jake's face registered a measure of relief, for he had half-expected the young man to pass away during the journey, rather than to regain consciousness.

'Who is Elly?' Jake asked. 'And who are you, and where are you from?'

The wounded man's face contorted

as he screwed his eyes and blinked several times, as if he was struggling hard to fight his way back to consciousness.

'Johnnie — Johnnie Parker — of the Rocking H ranch,' he stammered. Then his eyes opened wide in alarm as he seemed to register that he was not where he expected to be, rather like a man awaking from a nightmare. 'Cage! It was Rubal Cage that shot me! What — what happened?'

Jake pursed his lips sympathetically. 'There is no easy way to tell you this, Johnnie. It looks like there was a stampede. And I am guessing that all of your friends were killed.'

The shock of the news almost seemed too much. 'How — did they die?'

'They were shot. I found eight bodies as well as you. They were all murdered.'

Johnnie's eyes fluttered. 'Who are you, mister?'

'Name's Jake Scudder.'

Johnnie shook his head as if trying to

shake himself awake. 'Well Jake, can you get me to the Rocking H? I have to tell — to tell . . . '

But the effort was too much. His eyes blinked shut and he slumped back into deep unconsciousness.

Jake eased him back to the ground. 'Well Johnnie, I don't know where this Rocking H of yours is, but I reckon that Tucksville is going to be the nearest town. I'll get you there, then we can see what help we can get. One thing is certain though — there are some murdering dogs out there that the law needs to know about.'

4

It took an entire day to reach Tucksville and it was late in the afternoon when they reached the town limit. Almost immediately Jake found himself surrounded by a gang of street urchins and a few of the loafers who seemed to inhabit every south-western town.

'What you got there, mister? A dead man?' queried one dirty-faced youngster of about ten years of age.

'Are you a bounty hunter?' asked another.

Jake shook his head. 'The answer is 'no' to both questions. I have an injured man here in need of urgent medical attention. Can you point me in the direction of the town doctor?'

A grizzled oldster chuckled. 'A sawbones? You won't find anyone like that in Tucksville. We used to have one but he died of too much drink. Reckon the town constable might be your best bet, especially if there's been a shooting.'

'Who's been shot?' called out a high-pitched voice from the back of the crowd.

'Watch out, mister, here comes old Eagle-eye McCaid,' squealed one of the urchins, as the crowd parted to allow a small, tubby man of about fifty with the thickest lensed wire-framed spectacles Jake had ever seen. He was dressed in a shirt buttoned up to the collar, but without a tie, a waistcoat that was also buttoned, but which strained over his paunch, and yet with a brace of blue steel Colts in holsters on his hips. Pinned to the waistcoat was a crudely made deputy constable badge.

'Who said that?' he shrieked, peering myopically to right and left at the crowd of urchins, loafers and busybodies. 'Let's have some respect for the law around here.' And then blinking up at Jake he snapped out a series of questions in his high-pitched voice.

'Who have you got there, mister? Is he dead or alive? Need any help?'

'He's wounded pretty badly, but he isn't dead,' Jake replied. 'He's a tough kid if you ask me. I come upon him and a whole parcel of other cowboys at Rattlesnake Pass. They'd been shot up and their whole herd stolen. Some coyote had been left behind and was trying to finish them all off when I came along. He threw some lead at me but wandered off when I played possum. The kid here told me his moniker was Johnnie Parker of some spread called the Rocking H. That was afore he passed out.' He shook his head. 'And that was about a whole day ago, so I'm mighty keen to get him to a doctor.'

The grizzled oldster who was hovering at Deputy McCaid's shoulder piped up again. 'I told you, mister. We ain't got a doctor.'

Deputy McCaid peered at the old loafer. 'That you, Bart Rumgay?' Then before the other could reply, he peered up at Jake Scudder. 'He's right there, stranger. We have no doctor, but Matt Brooks, the town constable, knows something of doctoring. He's dug out enough bullets in his time.'

'Fortunately, the bullets didn't stay in Johnnie Parker here,' replied Jake, 'but I'd sure like another opinion on what we can best do for him.'

'Follow me then, Mr . . . '

'Scudder. Jake Scudder.'

Deputy McCaid coughed. 'OK, Mr Scudder, follow me to the jailhouse and we'll bed Johnnie Parker down in the spare cell. What did you say you did about the others?'

'The bodies are in a gully. Eight of them. I covered them up until you can go and recover them, then you can get after those murdering dogs.'

McCaid walked ahead while Jake and the assembled crowd of onlookers followed. 'We'll bring the bodies back, I reckon,' he said. 'But I don't know what Matt Brooks will say about going after those cattle-thieves.'

★ ★ ★

Jake Scudder's impression of Constable Matt Brooks was initially favourable. Clearly, the man had a strong physical presence and engendered confidence. He was tall, well-groomed and looked capable with both his fists and his sidearm. As soon as he saw the wounded man he showed his ability to organize by booming out a string of clipped orders.

'You two,' he barked to a couple of the surrounding loafers, 'Go into the back of the jailhouse and get some water boiling.' Then to Deputy McCaid, 'Samuel, go over to Joe Metcalf's emporium and get a couple of fresh blankets and some linen for bandages. Tell Joe the town will reimburse him.' And then to Scudder: 'If you'll help me in with the victim there, then I'll do what I can for him.'

Together they eased Johnnie Parker on to the wooden bunk in the spare cell. Then, when they had made him as comfortable as possible, Jake gave an account of how he had found the young man.

Matt Brooks stood up, a troubled frown upon his brow. 'It all leaves a bad taste in your mouth, right enough. And the poor kid has been unconscious for a whole day, you say. That's not a good sign.'

'But he seems a tough kid. I half-suspected that he wouldn't make the journey back here. Do you know him, Constable?'

Matt Brooks nodded. 'He's one of the Rocking H crew. I'll send a rider over to the ranch right away. It'll take a few hours.'

Jake nodded. 'And I guess you'll be sending a posse after the rustlers?'

To his surprise Matt Brooks shook his head. 'That is out of my jurisdiction, mister.' Then when he saw Jake's jaw drop in disbelief he continued: 'Oh, I'll send some boys out with the undertaker and his wagon to bring back the bodies, if you'll just give me a full description of exactly where in Rattlesnake Pass you found them. But as for going after rustlers, my hands are tied. My jurisdiction goes no further than the town boundary. I am a town constable, not a marshal.'

'But there's been a massacre out there!' Jake exclaimed. He was about to launch into a tirade towards the constable when Johnnie Parker stirred. Then he coughed and spluttered and his eyes flickered as he struggled back to consciousness.

* * *

Despite the constable's protestations about its not being necessary, Jake insisted upon staying to help look after the wounded Johnnie Parker as he drifted in and out of consciousness.

Samuel McCaid the deputy was ever ready to fetch meals and coffees and take his stint at mopping the perspiration from Johnnie's brow, and in so doing endeared himself to Jake. It seemed clear that he was a genuinely caring man who was something of an object of ridicule within the town, on account of his visual limitations and his resultant clumsiness.

When Matt Brooks was out on some business the deputy confided in Jake. 'I told you Matt wouldn't be too keen on chasing rustlers through Rattlesnake Pass.'

'Is the town constable a tad scared?' Jake ventured.

McCaid's eyes seemed to grow to three times their normal size behind his pebble-glass spectacles. 'Matt Brooks — scared? Hell no, Mr Scudder. He's just kind of — rigid. He won't do anything against the law. He lives for the letter of the law and the law says that his jurisdiction stops at the town's boundaries.'

Jake nodded and sipped his coffee. 'Then I reckon the law is some kind of an ass. Eight men were slaughtered out there in Rattlesnake Pass and the law surely has a duty to make sure they are brought to account.'

Deputy McCaid hung his head. 'I see that, and I truly wish I could do something about it.' Then he looked up, steely grit in his voice. 'But if those mongrels ever find their way into Tucksville, you can be sure that Matt Brooks will bring them to account, and no mistake!'

★   ★   ★

Light was fading outside and Deputy McCaid had lit the oil-lamps in the jailhouse before heading off for some food. Matt Brooks was writing reports at his desk and Jake was dozing beside the patient's bunk when he was startled awake by the sound of a buckboard being drawn to an abrupt halt outside the jailhouse. Stifling a yawn, Jake was rubbing the sleep from his eyes when the door burst open and a vision of determined loveliness, with long corn-coloured hair, dressed in men's range clothes, her hat hanging down her back, bustled into the constable's office. She was followed a step later by a tall man who moved with the grace of a puma, and whose Mexican clothes belied, in Jake's opinion, at least partial Apache ancestry.

'Miss Horrocks!' said Matt Brooks, rising swiftly from behind his desk. 'I thought that someone would be coming from the Rocking H, but not you. And not so quick.'

'El . . . Elly! Is that — you?' sighed Johnnie Parker, weakly raising himself on his elbows.

Before Matt Brooks could do anything, she was through the open door and clasping the wounded man's hands in hers. Jake immediately recognized the love that flowed between them. Awkwardly, he rose and backed out of the cell to give them some privacy.

He and the constable were drinking coffee and smoking quirlies while Yucatan stood impassively by the door when Elly Horrocks came into the office a few minutes later.

'I am taking Johnnie home now,' she

73

announced in a no-nonsense manner. 'Yucatan will drive us back.'

'But — ' began Matt Brooks.

'I reckon maybe I better come with you, ma'am,' Jake interjected. He gave the constable a brief, cold glance. 'Your ranch lost eight men. I guess your menfolk back at the ranch maybe want to talk to me.'

Elly Horrocks fixed him with a look that seemed a curious mix of amusement and pique, although Jake could not place which. But before he could say anything she nodded. 'Johnnie told me something of you, Mr Scudder. I and the menfolk would be very pleased for you to come back with us.'

★   ★   ★

On the way back to the Rocking H ranch Jake had little opportunity to discuss what had happened. Elly Horrocks rode in the buckboard with Johnnie Parker, who had been provided with a makeshift mattress, courtesy of

Joe Metcalf's emporium, while the taciturn Yucatan sat up front. The tall Mexican had, by his body language, made it clear that Jake was not welcome to sit on the buckboard bench alongside him. Accordingly, Jake trotted behind on his big black stallion.

Upon arriving at the Rocking H Jake quickly realized that it was a ranch beset with the deepest troubles. His initial assessment, however, was found to be an underestimation of just how bad things were when he sat with Elly and Saul after they had settled Johnnie Parker into the guest bedroom at the back of the ranch house. For one thing he had not realized that the remaining menfolk of the ranch consisted of Saul and Yucatan. He certainly had been surprised to find that Saul was confined to a wheelchair, having been shot in the same bush-whacking that had killed their father.

'I surely am sorry about the men who have all been killed,' he said, as he accepted a glass of whiskey from the reserved yet ever present Yucatan. 'But surely they weren't the entire crew of the Rocking H?'

'They were more than that,' replied Saul Horrocks as he sat nursing his own whiskey glass. 'We had hired more men for the drive. Now all that remains of the Rocking H is right here in this room — and Johnnie Parker through there.' He tossed back the remains of his drink, then gestured Yucatan to replenish it from the decanter atop the roll-top desk.

'Then you truly are in trouble,' mused Jake. He covered his glass as Yucatan made to refill it. 'So it looks as if you need all the help that you can get. Do you mind telling me how things got this way? Clearly, there's got to be some history to this tragedy.'

Between them, Elly and Saul filled Jake in.

'It is Elly that matters most to me,' Saul said, after they had described the run of bad luck that they had had over the last few years. 'I was a drinker, a waster and a bit of a wild thing. I feel bad about it now, but I took off and had me more adventures than I care to think about.' He grinned boyishly for a moment. 'And a good thing that I met my friend Yucatan there, during those wild days, or else I wouldn't be alive today. Anyway, my pa took me back in, welcomed me like the prodigal that I was — and now I am head of a ranch with no crew and only half a herd and a colossal debt to the bank. What hope have we got, Scudder? All that's left of us is me, a cripple, my little sister there, a half-dead wrangler and Yucatan.'

Elly Horrocks took a sip from her glass of lemonade. 'We will be all right, Saul,' she said, reassuringly.

Her brother stared at her uncomprehendingly, then his cheeks suffused with colour. 'All right? Tell me how, Elly? We're finished, can't you see that?' His voice rose in volume, simultaneously with an expression of increasing consternation on his face. 'We're finished! Might as well — '

He suddenly smashed the glass on the arm of his Bath chair and raised it above his head, as if to stab the paralysed legs that he obviously hated so much.

'No!' cried Elly.

Jake was out of his chair in a flash as Yucatan called out and took a step forward in similar fashion. Jake dashed a hand out and grasped Saul's fast descending wrist.

'Nothing to be gained by goring your legs, my friend,' Jake said calmly, as he removed the broken glass from Saul's hand.

Saul Horrocks stared at him like a man confused. 'What — what can we do then?' he asked helplessly.

'We can get our herd back!' replied Elly. 'And that is exactly what I am going to do.'

Saul stared at his sister in disbelief. 'What do you mean, Elly? How? You know yourself that Matt Brooks said he can't do anything.'

Jake Scudder sniffed sarcastically. 'He

said he won't do anything, you mean. He said it was out of his jurisdiction.'

'What did you mean, Elly?' Saul persisted. 'I am useless and there is nothing that a girl like you could — '

The torrent that greeted him took all of the men in the room by surprise. Elly Horrocks had shot to her feet in an instant, her arms akimbo and her jaw set. 'There is a great deal that *this* girl can and will do, brother dear! There is Horrocks blood flowing through these veins of mine, just as there is through yours. Our family have never been quitters. None of us! And I am not quitting on you now!'

Saul shook his head, tears visibly forming in his eyes. 'Elly, I swear, I never meant anything — offensive. I never meant that you were less than a man. You have your legs and that's more than I have. I just meant that — '

'You meant that a girl couldn't possibly do a man's job,' Elly returned, her voice calm, yet challenging.

Jake Scudder had been watching the

scene with ever-increasing admiration for Elly Horrocks. Spirit was a word that didn't come close, in his opinion, to describe the courage and resolve that she was displaying.

Yucatan seemed to have been forming the same opinion. He stepped forward. 'Miss Elly must not even think of going after these men. They are bad, vicious killers. I will go after them.'

Elly shook her head, her cheeks quite flushed now. 'Oh no you won't, Yucatan. You must stay here to look after Saul — and Johnnie. He needs all the help he can get to recover. And we all know how skilfully you nursed Saul back to health after he was wounded in the back.'

Saul was recovering himself. 'Then we should send out to Jeb Jackson's Double J ranch, and ask him to send us a few men to help.' He gave his sister a wan smile. 'Jeb would be only too happy to assist us, Elly.'

This suggestion was treated with disdain by Saul's sister. 'That is the last thing that is going to happen. I am surprised that you could even suggest such a thing, Saul — after everything that happened on that day. I will never ask for that man's help!'

Saul hung his head. 'That's it then. We have no option; we'll have to meet with the bank. Throw ourselves on their mercy.' His head shot up again, concern on his face. 'But one thing is definite, Elly. You can't go. I won't hear of it. I will — '

Jake Scudder suddenly laughed and clapped his hands. 'I have to say, Miss Horrocks, that you have as much spirit as any ten men. I salute your intention, but have you any idea of what is involved here? Have you any idea where they've taken your herd? How are you going to get your property back? Just ask them nicely?'

Elly looked at him and flushed. 'Why, I thought — '

'Have you ever shot at a rattlesnake? At a man?'

'No, of course I haven't.'

'Then you are going to need back-up. By rights that should be the law, but for some reason your local lawman doesn't see it that way.'

Saul Horrocks stared at Jake in disbelief. 'Are you saying you'll help, Mr Scudder? Why should you do that? This isn't your problem.'

Jake shrugged. 'Let's just say that I hate cold-blooded murder. And one of those jaspers shot at me. I reckon I have good reason to go along with your sister — if she'll let me tag along, that is.'

5

Although he admired Elly's pluck, Jake Scudder felt uneasy on several counts as they followed the trail that the herd had taken. For one thing he was conscious that as they approached Rattlesnake Pass they could easily be picked off by a rifleman hiding up in the Pintos. For another thing there were just the two of them, a man and an attractive woman. He wondered if that in itself was enough to unsettle her. If so, he wondered how he could best reassure her that she was safe with him. Although he had lived among some of the roughest *hombres* alive, Jake still maintained a strong sense of propriety. He realized all too well that sharing a camp with her was bound to compromise either her sense of privacy, which he respected, or his ability to guarantee her safety. And it was the latter that really troubled him, for he had given her brother his solemn oath that he would look after her.

'You needn't worry, Mr Scudder, I will not try to seduce you by moonlight,' said Elly suddenly, as if she had been reading his thoughts as they approached the entrance to Rattlesnake Pass.

Jake stared at her in amazement. 'Why, ma'am, how did you know what I was thinking?'

Elly chuckled. 'From everything that Johnnie told me and from what I have seen of you myself, as well as the way you talk,' she replied. 'I could see that you were looking worried, Mr Scudder.' She patted Trixie, her cowpony, then laughed when the pony neighed at her. Jake smiled at her laugh, for it was a musical laugh that showed him that beneath the strain that she was clearly under, she was a young woman capable of humour. 'I even think that Trixie here has been having similar thoughts about your stallion.'

Scudder grinned, his cheeks colouring slightly as the stallion suddenly shook its great head.

'See, I was right, wasn't I?' Elly asked. 'But you need not worry. I am spoken for. Johnnie and I are going to get married once we sort all this out — despite what my brother Saul thinks. So you are quite safe!' And at a touch of her knees and a click of her tongue the little cowpony trotted off ahead.

The big stallion swiftly caught her up. 'I sure am glad that we have cleared all that up, ma'am,' said Scudder. He grinned down at her. 'But how about it if we dropped the formality a mite. I am never very comfortable when I am tagged with the 'mister' label.

'OK, Jake — and I am Elly, remember.'

And as they rode together Jake pointed to a series of fresh wheel tracks and hoof prints in the sand. 'It looks as if a wagon came one way with a couple of riders, then went back again with a heavy load.'

Elly stammered: 'Y . . . you mean . . . ?'

Jake nodded at her unfinished question. 'I reckon that Constable Brooks sent the local undertaker and a couple of men out to Rattlesnake Pass ahead of us. It looks as if they've already recovered the bodies and taken them back to Tucksville.

And indeed, when they eventually approached the hollow in Rattlesnake Pass, Elly insisted upon seeing for herself where the Rocking H crew had met their end, the hellhole from which Jake had saved Johnnie Parker.

Jake saw Elly quaver in her saddle and he reached across, fearful that she might suddenly faint and topple from her saddle. But she was made of tougher stuff than that. She reached into her saddlebag and pulled out a small silver whiskey flask.

'Johnnie gave me this,' she explained, taking a sip and offering the flask to Jake.

Jake took the flask and raised it in the direction of the hollow, as if to toast the spirits of the dead cowboys. 'Here is hoping that we can make sure that you didn't all die in vain.'

★ ★ ★

Silver City was a typical railhead town, complete with pen-yards, cattle market, rail station and all the trappings that these involved; water-tower, coal-dump, log-warehouse, sidings, turning-circle and repair houses. The 'city' sobriquet had come when 'decent' folk arrived and the town quickly polarized into a working end and a society end. The society end meant it was the part of the town where the respectable families lived: the grocers, printers, lawyers, doctors and other bastions of respectability. The real 'social' scene, however, where one could find the saloons, cathouses and drug-dens, occupied a sort of unnamed and unspoken about (by the respectable women) hinterland to the east of the city. The defining name of the city — Silver — rightly

87

referred to the richness of the pickings in the city — which naturally appertained to all parts of the city.

Upon entering Silver City Jake and Elly naturally passed through the cattleyards and the railhead, only to find that the last train had headed north, laden with stock only the day before. Accordingly, the stock-pens were empty, the cattle having been transferred to the slaughter-yards in the north, while the pen-men had scattered to the entertainment part of town. All of the attached offices were locked up.

'I guess we had better check into a hotel first and then contact the local law,' Jake suggested.

Half an hour later, when they had found the sheriff's office, Elly knocked on the door and immediately entered, waking a bleary-eyed deputy from a whiskey-induced slumber. He had been slumped over the desk in the office, his head cradled on one forearm. He snapped himself upright at the sight of a lady, his expression one of confusion.

'What can I do for you, ma'am?' he asked as he rubbed sleep from his eyes then ran a hand over his dark stubbly jowl.

'I would appreciate a word with your sheriff,' Elly returned. 'It is about a robbery — rustling to be precise — a whole herd stolen.' She eyed the deputy sternly, as if to ensure that he was listening closely. 'But worse than that — eight good men were murdered. My whole crew.'

The deputy blinked repeatedly, as if he was forcing his brain to take in this information. 'M . . . Murder, did you say, ma'am? The sheriff will need to hear about this.'

'Then where is he?' demanded Jake, stepping past Elly and planting his palms forcefully on the desk, making all of the papers scatter and the deputy's elbows shudder.

'In . . . in the Busted Flush saloon,' the deputy stammered, his Adam's apple bobbing up and down nervously at sight of the big puncher eyeing him belligerently.

'We'll go and flush him out then,' said Jake, straightening up, and tipping his hat. 'Appreciate your help, Deputy. Guess we'll probably meet up again.'

Deputy Hank Bott hoped not. But when the tall cowboy and the pretty lady left, a sly grin spread across his dark jowls. 'And maybe you won't be seeing many more people anyways, my friend,' he said softly to himself. 'Not if you adopt that attitude around the sheriff.' And then his thoughts turned lasciviously towards the pretty woman accompanying him. 'But maybe you'll meet a lot of fellers who take a shine to you, ma'am. Especially if you go into the Busted Flush.'

★   ★   ★

The Busted Flush saloon was the 'superior' saloon in Silver City. It boasted gaming tables, a faro wheel and the prettiest chorus line west of the Pintos. And to top it all it was run by Carmen de Menendez, reckoned by most of the *cognoscenti* to be the best-looking saloon-owner in the southwest. She was said to be a Mexican lady of good lineage, able to trace her family back to the *caballeros* of Old Spain. As for her 'girls', they were all chosen for their looks, if not their morals.

The décor of the saloon had a decidedly Mexican feel. That was not to say that it was like any of the cantinas found around the borders, rather that it had an ambience of gentility and of Hispanic opulence.

The bartenders all had thick, lush moustaches, wore flamboyant, wide-sleeved shirts, with multi-coloured bandannas about their necks. The mirrors behind the long bar were of fine gilt, and dotted about the walls were brightly coloured pictures of dancing *señoritas* and white toothed *vaqueros*.

A piano-player was tinkling away below the raised stage, across which the curtains had been drawn, presumably in a break between chorus-line numbers. The square dance area was similarly free. Apart from that, the saloon was already pretty well packed and the air was thick with a tobacco haze. Saloon-girls dashed between tables dexterously carrying trays of beer and whiskey, while others just stood by various punters 'for luck'. Every now and then some lucky gambler would gather in his winnings and leave the game to reward his luck-bringer in one or other of the upstairs rooms.

Elly took no notice of the curious stares that she and Scudder received from the clientele, the saloon-girls and the bar staff. She strode purposefully towards the bar where a swarthy, grinning bartender was polishing glasses.

'We are looking for the sheriff,' Jake said.

The bartender laughed. 'An unusual request, *señor*. Most people in Silver City prefer not to meet the sheriff.' And then seeing that neither Elly nor Jake saw any humour in his remark he pointed to the far corner of the saloon where a card-game was going on.

'Sheriff Slim Parfitt is right over there playing poker with the boss, Miss Carmen de Menendez.'

Weaving their way through the crowd they made their way to the card-table where five people were playing. They stood waiting for an opportunity to interrupt the play.

The sheriff's sobriquet of 'Slim' was far from apt, since he was a man of more than ample girth, with at least two chins. His clothes hugged him and their aged look suggested that he had slowly been expanding in width. As he sat cradling his cards a thin film of perspiration covered his face and his receding hairline. Bloodshot eyes and a half-consumed bottle of whiskey at his elbow indicated a fondness for liquor. As Jake watched him he wondered whether his perspiration was due to his physical condition or to his gambling prowess, or lack of it.

Across the table from the sheriff sat a woman of remarkable beauty. Olive-skinned, full ruby-red lips and raven-black hair, she was dressed in a yellow silk dress that revealed her feminine curves to perfection. About her neck was a black choker that favourably emphasized her long neck. Unlike the sheriff she seemed to be the very personification of calmness. No one would have any idea of what sort of hand she held from the expression on her face.

And there was a sizeable pot in the centre of the table. As the game went on the other three players caved in, leaving only the sheriff and the saloon-owner. Eventually the sheriff took a gulp of whiskcy from his glass, belched loudly and then threw a fistful of dollar bills into the pot. 'Think I'll see you, Carmen. There's no way you're going to beat my hand today.'

Only then did Carmen de Menendez speak. 'Let's see, Slim,' she said, laying her cards down one by one. 'Only, how do you think you can beat four aces?'

The sheriff stared in wide-eyed disbelief, then tossed his cards down and guffawed. 'Darn! That cleans me out again. The least you could do is buy me a drink.'

But Elly could keep quiet no longer. 'Am I seeing things, or are you the sheriff of Silver City?' she asked, her eyes smouldering and her jaw set firm. 'What sort of a law officer can be drinking and gambling at this time of the day when he should be on duty.'

Sheriff Parfitt was not one to sit and take insults from anyone, yet as he turned his bleary eyes on Elly he was all too conscious of the tall, capable-looking man with a tied-down Remington, standing at her right side. 'Something troubling you, ma'am?' he asked.

'There certainly is. I have been robbed. A whole herd belonging to the Rocking H ranch was stolen and my men were murdered. Massacred!'

Carmen de Menendez gasped. 'But that is terrible. When did this awful thing happen, Miss . . . ?'

Elly tore her eyes away from the sheriff. 'Horrocks. Elly Horrocks. It happened at Rattlesnake Pass a couple of days ago.'

The Silver City sheriff shrugged his shoulders. 'So why are you telling me? Rattlesnake Pass is nothing to do with me.'

Jake had been quiet till now, but felt his hackles rise. 'What is it with lawmen in this part of the country? They don't seem to care about what happens outside their towns. Now look here, you miserable piece of — '

Slim Parfitt sat forward, his face hardening. 'Now you just back off, mister. I don't take kindly to — '

Carmen de Menendez suddenly stood up. 'Sheriff Slim, perhaps the least you could do is to hear the lady out.' She turned and smiled at Elly. 'My name is Carmen de Menendez. I own the Busted Flush and I think it would be a good idea, perhaps, if we all adjourned to my private office.'

Without more ado she led the way through the saloon, past an alcove where Hog Fleming, Cole Lancing and Rubal Cage were drinking whiskey, each with a saloon-girl on his knees.

Rubal Cage had been listening to the exchange with great interest. He smacked his girl on her butt, much to her irritation, and stood up.

'Where you going, Rubal?' the porcine Hog Fleming asked.

Rubal Cage frowned. 'I reckon we've got business that might need attending to. Come outside and let's get some fresh air. I'll tell you what you need to do.'

★ ★ ★

Carmen de Menendez handed Elly and Jake glasses of wine while Sheriff Parfitt helped himself to a sizeable measure of whiskey from a decanter on a side-table in the office.

Elly described all that had happened and Jake told them about his encounter with the man who had been cold-bloodedly shooting the bodies in the gully.

'In my opinion, you won't find any of these men this side of the Pintos by now,' said the sheriff.

'That means it is likely that they sold the herd here in Silver City,' said Elly. 'And in that case, there will be a record of the transaction.'

Slim Parfitt nodded. 'Guess so. The cattle buyer for C & SW, the Central and South-West Cattle Company, will have it all documented.'

'Will you take me to see him, Sheriff?' Elly asked.

The lawman seemed to hesitate, but on prompting from Carmen de Menendez he heaved himself to his feet. 'I reckon I can do that.'

Elly looked at Jake. 'Will you come too?'

Scudder shook his head. 'No, ma'am. You and the sheriff can do that just fine. I think I will maybe have another drink in the bar before I head back to the hotel and clean up.'

Two patches of colour formed on Elly's cheeks, but she said nothing more. Instead, she nodded to Carmen de Menendez and followed the sheriff out.

Once they had gone, Carmen de Menendez shook her head. 'I am afraid for your friend. I have my doubts that she will get her herd or her money back.'

Jake drained his wine and laid it on the table. 'I must say, I had much the same thought. Thank you for the wine and hospitality, ma'am.' He smiled. 'It isn't exactly my kind of drink though, so I think I'll have a beer and then go clean up.'

She smiled at him. 'You'll find this one of the best saloons, Mr Scudder. Enjoy yourself while you are here.'

The piano-player began to play just as Jake put a hand on the door handle, and a moment later the sound of the chorus-line started up, to much raucous laughter. 'You know, ma'am. It sounds a fun place, right enough. I think I may just do that.'

★　★　★

Elly Horrocks felt frustrated. Sheriff Slim Parfitt had sent his deputy Hank

Bott to find and bring the C & SW Cattle Company agent to his office. To her dismay she was shown the documentation in the ledger confirming the sale of the Rocking H stock to the C & SW Cattle Company.

'There you are ma'am,' said Nat Tooking, the myopic cattle agent over the top of his half-moon spectacles. 'All legally signed, witnessed and dated. There's your representative, Bill Coburn's signature.'

Elly had gone pale at sight of the clear, but patently forged signature. 'But that isn't Bill's signature,' she protested. 'He was lying dead in Rattlesnake Pass when whoever signed that.'

Nat Tooking looked at her in amazement. 'Did you say he was dead? What are you saying, ma'am?'

Sheriff Parfitt interrupted. 'It looks as if you were duped, Nat.'

The cattle agent stared at the ledger for a moment, then he emphatically shook his head. 'No way! I paid good dollar in good faith for that herd. How do I know that this lady is telling the truth?'

Elly felt her temper rise. 'How dare you. All of my crew have been murdered and my — my fiancé is lying seriously wounded at our ranch.' She stabbed the ledger with a finger. 'This deception is illegal and we shall insist on being reimbursed.'

Nat Tooking's lips had twisted into a sneer of contempt. 'I can assure you, ma'am, that the C & SW Cattle Company will not pay out twice.'

Sheriff Parfitt raised his hand. 'And before you say anything more, ma'am — this rustling that you allege is totally out of my jurisdiction. Rattlesnake Pass and anything that happens there is nothing whatever to do with Silver City or with me.'

Elly glared at him. 'How did I know you were going to say something like that?' she asked sarcastically. She bid the two men good-day, then strode out of the office and crossed the street to the Silver City Classic Hotel, where she and Scudder had booked rooms earlier.

It was not until she was alone in her room with the door closed and locked that she sank on to the bed, covered her face and dissolved into tears.

6

Elly was not in her room when Jake got back to the hotel, so he cleaned up then went for a walk in order to think things over. He strolled around the town to try and get a feel for the place. But something kept telling him that the most likely place he'd get answers would be the Busted Flush. By the time he pushed the batwing doors open again it was dark outside and the chandeliers had been lit, making it seem even more inviting.

He ordered a beer with a whiskey chaser from the same bartender who had directed Elly and himself to the card-game where they met the sheriff and Carmen de Menendez. After paying and chatting for a few moments he headed towards a spare table in an alcove. Like a wasp honing in on a honeypot, he was soon joined by an attractive young woman in a gaudy and slightly ill-fitting purple dress.

'Need some company, mister?' she asked, taking a draw on a thin quirly that she held between her second and third fingers. Almost immediately she bent over with a rasping cough. 'The name is Rosalind,' she said, recovering quickly and colouring with embarrassment.

Jake indicated the chair beside him. 'Be glad of it, Rosalind,' he replied. Then pointing to her cigarette: 'You are mighty young to have a cough as bad as that. Those gaspers are not good for the lungs, you know.'

'Preacherman, are you?' she returned coyly, raising an eyebrow with mock sarcasm.

Scudder shook his head. 'Just a simple man with simple tastes.'

She giggled. 'That's not the way most men talk when they come to the Busted Flush. Some of them have very . . . complicated . . . tastes. Care to buy me a drink?'

Jake signalled to the nearest bartender who sent another smiling saloon-girl over with a tray and Rosalind's 'usual', a mint julep. She sipped it, took another puff on her acrid quirly and coughed again.

Jake shook his head. 'How old are you, Rosalind?'

'Twenty,' she replied swiftly.

'More like sixteen or seventeen, I reckon.' He reached over, removed the quirly from her hand and ground it on the floor under his heel. 'Come on, I think some fresh air would do you more good than that drink and those coffin nails.'

Rosalind shook her head vigorously. 'But I can't. I have to — '

'Yes you can,' Jake replied. 'I'll pay you for your time. All I want is to just walk around a little. Have a chat.'

And without further protestations Rosalind felt herself being gently propelled through the busy saloon and out of the batwing doors onto the boardwalk.

'A walk in the moonlight, how romantic,' she giggled.

'Tell me about yourself, Rosalind. Where are you from?'

One thing about Rosalind was clear. She could talk. By the time they had strolled to the end of a long boardwalk she had told him what he was sure was a pack of lies. She claimed to have been at college back east, to have fallen in love with an engineer and to have come west with him.

He proffered his arm as they stepped down from the boardwalk into the dusty street and began to cross the mouth of a darkened alleyway.

'But then he had an accident and I — '

Neither of them had expected the burst of activity to erupt from the darkened alley. Jake heard a rustling noise and immediately moved sidewards. His right hand darted for his Remington. But he had started at too much of a disadvantage. Before he could clear leather he felt a searing pain on the top of his right shoulder, which shot down his arm. Instantly, he realized that he had been struck a glancing blow with some kind of bludgeon that had been meant to kill rather than just maim. With his right arm temporarily out of commission he knew that he was vulnerable.

As was Rosalind! Jake heard her scream, and chancing a glance to his left he saw a man wearing a bandanna over his face dragging her into the alleyway.

Another flurry of movement alerted him to the fact that his own assailant had gathered himself together and was in the act of reattempting to stave in his head. He could not dodge aside again, so he dropped, and at the same time threw himself sideways, sweeping his legs in a scissors movement. He made contact and heard a howl as a body fell on top of his legs. Immediately, Jake grabbed the plank of wood that had been used on him and wrenched it free with his left hand.

The assailant rolled free and leapt to

his feet, a hand reaching for a gun at his side. Jake lashed out with the plank and caught the man's gun hand before he could draw the weapon. Then, as the other cried in pain, he changed the direction of his swing and struck for all he was worth at the man's groin. There was a shriek of pain, then a rasped command. Jake could not make out what name the man called out, but it was clear that it was a cry for help from the other.

Jake was struggling to his feet when Rosalind was thrown at him and he was bowled over onto his back, with her landing on top of him. He shoved her gently aside, his right arm now reflexly going for the Remington at his side. It came up, not quite as smoothly as usual, and he let off two shots in the direction of the two assailants as they departed into the greater darkness.

Then all he was aware of was Rosalind, sobbing beside him.

'Oh God! Take me away from this, mister. I want my . . . ' she moaned, pressing herself against his chest. 'Please take me away from this miserable life.'

Predictably, when gunshots sounded out in the darkness there was a slow build-up of commotion. No one rushed to investigate, for fear of catching a stray bullet, but gradually the curious edged along the boardwalk until the source of the shooting was located. Then the muttering and mumbling became louder as rumour and slow seepage of fact merged into one another, and a crowd began to form around the entrance to the alley.

'Anyone hurt?' cried one voice.

'Dunno,' yelled another. 'Bring some light.'

There was a snort, and then a dismissive voice reported, 'It's just a guy and a whore.'

Jake was standing with his arm about Rosalind's shoulders. She was trembling like a little girl and he snapped in the direction of the last anonymous speaker. 'Whoever said that had better

109

keep his mouth shut afore I shove a cake of soap in it. This lady has had a bad shock — after a couple of the low life in this town tried to jump us.' He worked his aching shoulder like a windmill and advanced on the crowd, which parted before him.

'Hold up there!' called a voice that Jake recognized as belonging to Sheriff Slim Parfitt. 'If there's been gunplay in Silver City I want to know who's been doing it.'

Jake and Rosalind had moved into the circle of light tossed out by one of the boardwalk lanterns. 'I fired, Sheriff — at a couple of cowardly curs who tried to sandbag us as we walked past that alley.'

The sheriff eyed Jake narrowly. 'What were you doing out here with this — lady? She's one of the girls from the Busted Flush, ain't she?'

'My name is Rosalind,' the girl returned with some spirit. 'And yes, I do work at the saloon for Miss Carmen. What of it? It is a good house, as you well know.'

'I didn't say it wasn't,' returned the sheriff, dismissively. Turning his attention to Jake he shook his head. 'You seem to attract trouble, mister. I don't like that in my town.'

Jake shrugged. 'Then if I were you — Sheriff — I'd start doing a proper sheriff job and clear the low life out of this town.' And before the lawman could remonstrate, he jabbed a finger towards him and demanded: 'Did you take care of Miss Horrocks?'

Slim Parfitt frowned. 'I introduced her to Nat Tooking, the C & SW Cattle Company agent, but it all looked above board to me. The herd had been bought and paid for. Last I saw of her she was headed back for the hotel.'

Jake nodded and moved off. 'I'll leave you to apprehend those dogs. Excuse us now, I have to see this lady gets home safe and sound.'

As they walked away from the fast dispersing crowd Rosalind held tightly to Jake's arm. 'Don't leave me, will you, mister. I am scared those two might come back.'

Jake patted the hand on his arm. He recognized that this was not the play of a saloon-girl anxious to hook a punter. She was terrified, and he suspected that she knew who the attackers were.

★ ★ ★

Carmen de Menendez rushed over from the bar when Jake brought Rosalind in through the batwing doors of the saloon. 'My God! Is Rosalind hurt?' she asked, her face full of concern. 'I heard those shots, but I didn't think — '

'I am OK, Miss Carmen,' Rosalind said with a tremulous smile. 'Mr Scudder here saved me from . . . ' she bit her lip, and then went on: 'from two horrible animals. It was so dark, I didn't see who they were.'

'I think she needs to lie down and rest awhile,' Jake said.

Rosalind tightened her grip on his

arm and looked up pleadingly. 'W . . . would you stay with me a while, Mr Scudder?'

'Of course I will,' Jake replied. Then to Carmen de Menendez. 'If that's all right with you, ma'am.'

The saloon-owner nodded understandingly. 'Of course. She's shocked, like you say. Go up and I'll have some drinks sent up.'

Jake was all too aware of the knowing looks that were being exchanged all around as he helped Rosalind up the stairs, and he ignored them. Once inside her room, however, she moved away from him and sat on the edge of her bed, at the edge of the circle of light thrown out from the oil-lamp by her bedside. She looked up, a half-smile on her trembling lips.

'I really am grateful, Mr Scudder,' she said, as she began to unfasten the front of her dress.

Jake waved a finger and shook his head. 'Just keep your clothes on, Rosalind. Like I said, I just want to talk to you. You don't need to thank me — and certainly not that way.' He looked about the Spartanly furnished room and sat down on the solitary chair in front of her dressing-table.

She looked crestfallen, hurt. 'But I — '

They were interrupted by a tap on the door. Jake crossed the room and threw open the door to find a young man with finely chiselled Apache features standing with a tray upon which were a bottle and a couple of glasses.

'Brandy for you and the young lady,' he announced, his expression totally impassive.

Casting a look at Rosalind, Jake took the tray and nodded. 'I think a little drink would do her some good.' He fished in his pocket and produced a few coins. 'What is your name, my friend?'

'Nantan,' replied the other, accepting the coins without obvious enthusiasm. Then with a nod, he said, 'thank you, sir.'

'What does it mean?' Jake persisted.

'In your language, '*he who speaks*'.' And with another nod he turned on his heel and left.

Jake closed the door with his foot and crossed the room to the dressing-table, where he poured two glasses of brandy. 'His name seems a bit of a joke,' he said with a grin. 'He seems kind of uninterested in everything, rather as if he'd prefer to be asleep.'

Rosalind smiled. 'Nantan? Yes, he's a strange one. He came into town about six months ago. He does any job that anyone will pay him to do. And you are right, I have never seen him smile or show any emotion.' She accepted the glass and drained it in one swallow, shaking her head as the liquid hit her stomach.

'You did need that, didn't you,' Jake said, sipping his brandy. 'Now tell me the truth, Rosalind. You went to pains to tell Carmen de Menendez that it was too dark to see those jaspers who attacked us.' He stared at her with penetrating eyes. 'But you knew them, didn't you?'

Rosalind dropped her head to avoid his regard. 'They — are — horrible,' she replied slowly, emphasizing each word. 'They are evil, Mr Scudder. They are violent — to women!'

'The curs!' Jake exclaimed. He held all women in the highest regard and felt disgust for those who did not. He swallowed his own brandy and topped up their glasses again.

Rosalind smiled and sipped her drink, then turned and nodded at the bed. 'Wouldn't you like to be more comfortable — Jake?'

Scudder reached over and patted the back of her hand. 'Rosalind, I still do not believe that you are as old as you say. And I do not think that your way of life is doing you any good. I do not want to sleep with you. In fact, I would like to stake you some money so that you can get away from here.'

Rosalind's eyes lit up for a moment. Then the light faded. 'I have had men say things like that before. All of the girls have, but nothing ever happens.'

'How long have you worked here, Rosalind?'

'A year. Miss Carmen is a good boss. She has been kind to me.'

Jake swallowed some more brandy, then yawned, suddenly feeling quite weary. 'And what about those men? You told me they were violent to women. Do you know anything else about them?' He blinked and rubbed his eyes.

Rosalind yawned as well, then took another drink. 'I declare you are making me feel sleepy, Jake,' she said coquettishly. 'They come and go. They have been in town before, then left for months. Cattlemen, they claim to be, but I think . . . '

'What do you think, Rosalind?'

'I think they — could be thieves,' she replied, stifling another yawn. 'Rustlers, maybe.'

Her eyes rolled upwards and she suddenly fell backwards on the bed, her brandy glass tumbling from her hand

and rolling across the floor.

Jake felt his head begin to swim and he rose unsteadily to his feet. 'I — kind of — feel groggy — too!' he murmured, staring suspiciously at his own half-empty glass. Then he staggered forward and collapsed on the bed beside Rosalind.

★ ★ ★

Nantan had done his job and then reported back to the cellar where he had been told to meet his boss.

'Did they seem suspicious about anything?' the boss demanded.

The impassive Nantan shook his head.

'And did you wait outside like I told you to?'

Nantan nodded again. 'I heard them talking. He asked a lot of questions and she answered. I could not make out all of her answers, except for one.'

'Go on!'

'She said she thought they were rustlers.'

'Anything else?'

'No, they fell asleep.'

The boss laughed. 'How do you know that?'

'There was the noise of them falling on the bed, then nothing more. Normally those beds make many spring noises, but not this time.'

'You are a prize, Nantan!' And several dollars passed from palm to palm.

* * *

Elly had wept for a while, and then pulled herself together, as was her way. She realized that things were looking bad for the Rocking H, but if she was to salvage anything from all this, it would be up to her. And that meant that she had to think straight.

'Where is Jake?' she asked herself again and again. And when he still hadn't appeared two hours later she lay down on the bed and tried to work out her next move. Almost mercifully she fell into a slumber. A slumber from which she was rudely awakened by the noise of two shots from somewhere not too far off.

She was awake instantly, her immediate concern being that the shots could have something to do with Jake Scudder. But then her reasoning mind took over and she realized that in a railhead town like Silver City, such shooting in the evening was probably related to some cowboy letting off steam, or to some gambler celebrating a win at the tables. Either way it was unlikely to have anything to do with Scudder. And so thinking she dozed off again, fully expecting Jake Scudder to appear at some point and waken her in the process.

She managed to fall into a deep sleep this time and was only dimly aware of a light tap at the door. After a few moments it was repeated by a louder and more persistent knocking.

'Who . . . who is it?'

'Scudder,' came the reply.

Elly rubbed her eyes as she slid off her bed and crossed to the door. 'Where have you been?' she asked as she undid the lock. 'I have been waiting for hours.'

She opened the door a few inches, then was surprised when it was forcefully pushed open.

'What the — ?' she began.

The black figure of Rubal Cage grinned at her. 'Actually, Scudder couldn't make it — so he sent me.'

Elly's mouth opened as if to emit a scream. But it never left her lips, for at that moment Rubal Cage's fist dashed up and caught her on the point of the chin, lifting her off the floor and propelling her backwards into the room, where she fell with a dull thud.

'Come on, you two,' Cage snapped as he entered the room.

When all three of them were inside, standing around the unconscious figure of Elly Horrocks, Hog Fleming kicked the door closed.

7

Jake woke with a thundering headache as a shaft of light from the new dawn shone through the chink in the cheap curtains. His tongue felt as though it was stuck to the roof of his mouth and he felt slightly nauseated. He was lying face down on the bed beside the form of a girl whose bosom gently rose and fell mere inches from his face.

'Rosalind,' he said softly, more to himself than to her, as he raised his head to gather his senses. He pushed himself up from the bed, stretching and working his shoulders to ease his aching muscles.

At the sound of her name, Rosalind awoke with a start. 'Wh ... what happened?' she asked in some confusion. 'Weren't we drinking . . . ?'

Jake had picked up the errant glass that had rolled across the floor and stood sniffing it. 'We were drinking drugged brandy,' he replied, his jaw setting in a look of grim determination. 'And I am going to find out who was responsible.'

Rosalind's eyes opened wide with alarm. 'Not Nantan?'

Jake shook his head. 'He delivered it, but it was sent up by your boss, Carmen de Menendez.'

Rosalind gave an emphatic shake of her head. 'Miss Carmen wouldn't do anything like that.'

Jake poured water from the washing-pitcher into the large porcelain bowl on the dressing-stand, then sluiced it over his face. He sniffed the pitcher to ensure that it too was not drugged and then took a hefty swig to clean his mouth.

'I reckon that at this moment the main question is, why were we drugged?'

'You don't think it could have been those two men?'

'That is possible, Rosalind,' Jake replied. He felt concerned for her, since she had clearly had a bad shock the night before. 'Now you can see why I think you need to get away from this way of life. It is not healthy.'

Rosalind bit her lower lip. 'But I cannot get away from it. I have no money.'

'I told you that I would stake you,' he returned. He pulled out a wad of notes from his back pocket and peeled a number off. 'This should be enough to buy a train ticket for as far as you want to go. I have some business to sort out first, then I'll come back later today and put you on a train myself.'

Rosalind stared incredulously at the money. 'You'll do that for me? But I have not done anything for you.'

Jake gave her a wry smile. 'Rosalind, I think it is time you showed some faith in the human race. Not everyone you meet is going to want something from you. I want you to look at this money as your second chance. Take it.'

And he reached for the door while Rosalind continued to stare in disbelief at the money. 'I will be ready, Jake.'

He nodded then left.

'I will never know how to thank you, Jake Scudder,' Rosalind whispered as she stared at the closed door.

★ ★ ★

Elly had woken during the night with a painful jaw and a splitting headache, from when her head had hit the bedroom floor and snuffed out her consciousness. For a moment she could not understand why her head was hanging down with her arms dangling on each side. Then she realized that she was in motion, being jolted up and down. She was unable to move either her hands or her feet and she realized that she had been slung over Trixie's saddle, and that her hands and feet were tied and a linking loop was knotted under Trixie's belly.

'Gah!' she exclaimed angrily. 'Who the hell did this?'

She was greeted by a chorus of

laughter from what she perceived to be three men riding alongside her.

'The girl can cuss,' said one voice.

'Maybe we got ourselves a whore and not a lady,' sneered another.

'Sure isn't going to matter which, anyhow,' growled a third.

Elly felt a sharp pain on her bottom, accompanied by the sound of a smack from the flat of the third voice's hand. Then the three men guffawed again.

'You will pay for that — all three of you!' Elly hissed defiantly. 'What do you want? Money?'

'Maybe a little more than money,' returned the third voice.

'You wouldn't dare!' Elly snapped, although she felt far less sure of herself than she sounded.

'We'll see,' said the first voice. 'It will be sun-up soon. Time for my two friends here to have a bit of a rest and maybe feed you some breakfast. As for me — I will see you after I attend to some business — in maybe a day or so.'

The horses had all stopped and Elly

heard the men whispering to one another as the sun began to rise over the cactus and red-boulder-strewn desert. She strained her ears to hear what was being said.

'Take her to the cabin to the west of Rattlesnake Pass,' said the leader. 'Wait a day then bring her along and meet me. Just remember what I told you, and don't let anyone get near you. If they do — kill them!'

Raising her head as much as she was able, Elly saw the leader spur his horse in a direction that she recognized to be towards Rattlesnake Pass.

'Come on then, lady,' said the second voice. 'I don't know about you, but I could sure eat some breakfast — first!'

★ ★ ★

Jake mounted the steps of the Silver City Classic Hotel three at a time and tapped on Elly's door. He waited for a few seconds, which he thought was respectful, and then knocked again, louder this time. 'Elly! Elly, I need to talk to you,' he called through the door.

He heard somebody grumble from a neighbouring room, but heard not a stir from Elly's room. He tried the handle and found it locked.

'What is the noise all about?' came a voice from behind him, and he spun round, his hand hovering above the handle of his Remington.

Joe Holland, the lame night porter, dishevelled and bleary-eyed from half a bottle of rye whiskey, staggered back a pace with his hands above his head. 'Don't shoot, mister. I'm just the night porter.' Then he blinked and recognized Jake from the evening before. 'That isn't your room, Mr Scudder. Your room is down the hall. That is the lady's room.' And as soon as he said it a lascivious look flashed across his face.

Jake spied the hotel master-key dangling from his belt. 'I know that, you darned fool!' he said, impatiently. 'I have a bad feeling — get that door open before I break it in!'

'I can't,' Holland replied. 'Every guest's room is private, so long as they have paid. It's hotel policy.'

Jake's hand curled over the handle of the Remington. 'I have just changed hotel policy. Now open that door. *Sabe!*'

Joe Holland's head bobbed up and down with alacrity as he tremulously shoved the key in the lock and opened the door with as much haste as he could muster.

'S . . . sorry, ma'am. I was made to,' he mumbled as he stood at the door. 'Why, it is empty!' he gasped. 'She . . . she has gone, Mr Scudder.'

'I can see that for myself,' replied Jake irritably, entering the room and looking round. 'All her things are here.' Then he spied a red patch on the floor and he bent to examine it. 'Blood!'

His eyes came up and fixed accusingly on Joe Holland. 'How come you let a guest get kidnapped?'

'K . . . kidnapped? No way, Mister Scudder. I was down there all evening.

Except for when I got that — '

Jake grabbed his shirt-front and pulled him close. 'When you got — what?' he thundered.

Joe Holland gulped. 'The message! I got a m . . . message to go over to the Busted Flush to see the sheriff.'

'What did he want?' Jake asked in exasperation.

'N . . . nothing, Mr Scudder. He . . . he wasn't there, after all.'

A look of worry crept over Jake's brow. 'Who brought you this message?'

'An Apache kid. Seen him around a lot, but I don't know his name. He does all kinds of odd jobs for folk.'

Jake shook his head. 'I don't suppose I can get hold of this sheriff of yours?'

'At this time of the morning? Not a chance, mister.'

Without another word Jake left the hotel and went straight to the livery stable. He had little difficulty in rousing the ostler, a middle-aged fellow who had sworn the oath against drinking.

'Where is Miss Horrocks's cowpony?' Jake asked, after informing him of his suspicions.

'A guy with a bandaged up ear took it out last night. He said he was taking her out to meet someone who knew something about her lost herd. The whole town has been buzzing about it. I thought it was all above board.'

'I don't suppose you know where they were headed?'

The ostler shook his head.

Jake frowned, then asked him to get his stallion ready. His best guess was that whoever had taken her wouldn't be heading north. Some instinct told him that they would be heading south, towards Rattlesnake Pass. Hurriedly he mounted the stallion, then he tossed a dollar to the ostler. With luck, he reckoned, he would be able to pick up the trail outside town. Elly's cow pony, Trixie, had pretty distinctive horseshoes — he hoped that he would find them.

★   ★   ★

Rosalind had washed and was applying make-up at her dressing-table when there came a soft tap on the door. Despite herself she stiffened as images of the men who attacked her and Scudder flashed before her mind's eye.

'It's OK, Rosalind, it is only me,' came Carmen de Menendez's lilting voice.

Rosalind heaved a sigh of relief, and then crossed the room to let her employer in.

Concern was written all over Carmen de Menendez's face. 'I just wanted to see that you were all right, Rosalind. I saw that Jake Scudder fellow leave as if his tail was on fire.'

Rosalind laughed girlishly. 'He was a perfect gentleman, Miss Carmen. But he was worried about his lady friend. That's why he took off like that.'

Then she realized that she had left the wad of money — an excessive amount of money for one night — lying on her bedside table. And she was sure that the saloon-owner had seen it too.

'A generous man,' said Carmen de Menendez, with a humourless smile, as if divining Rosalind's thoughts.

'I . . . I — ' began Rosalind.

'You what?' asked Carmen de Menendez, reaching out and stroking Rosalind's hair. 'Tell me what, my dear.'

Suddenly, Rosalind felt pain as Carmen de Menendez grabbed her hair and cruelly yanked her head backwards. 'Tell me, you little bitch!' she hissed. 'Why did he give you so much money? What did you tell him?'

'N . . . nothing, Miss Carmen. I swear. Nothing!' Her eyes were wide with terror as she saw the reflection in the dresser-mirror; of her with her head pulled back and her throat exposed, and Miss Carmen staring at her with a look of stark animal fury.

'That is just as well,' the saloon-owner said between gritted teeth, as she tightened her grip on Rosalind's hair.

A scream threatened to erupt from Rosalind's lips as she saw Carmen de

Menendez reach across the dressing-table and pick up her long scissors.

'No! No, Miss Carmen, please,' she begged. 'Don't cut my hair, please.'

A smile that was almost reptilian marred the beautiful saloon-owner's face, and she shook her head. 'What made you think I would touch your hair, my dear?'

Again the scream threatened to erupt from Rosalind's lips as she saw the flash of steel in the mirror. But a moment later blood splattered the mirror, blotting out the image of her pitifully silent, terrible death.

★   ★   ★

It was late morning by the time Jake Scudder confirmed in his own mind that the trail he was following was indeed leading towards Rattlesnake Pass. There were three horses and Elly's cowpony, and they were clearly following a back trail, rather than the main way towards the Pintos.

'Those devils better not have harmed a hair on her head,' he mused to the back of the stallion's head. Then he cursed himself for being caught out by that drugged brandy. 'Maybe I should have waited and gotten that no-account sheriff and his deputy to come too. Three of these rustling *hombres* may be hard to handle.'

He urged the stallion onwards towards the pass, trying hard to pick the tracks of the kidnappers from the churned up floor of the pass, which still bore the evidence of the stampede of three days before.

Then behind him he heard the cadence of rapidly approaching hoofs and the whooping and bawling of a group of men. The noise seemed typical of a group under the influence of more than a little tonsil paint. Jake wheeled the stallion round and waited for them to turn the last bend. He rested his hands on the pommel of his Texas rig as he recognized two of the men — the Silver City sheriff and his deputy. Both of them were swaying slightly, as were another three riders, while another rode calmly and impassively by their side. This man he also recognized — it was the young Apache, Nantan.

'You look like a posse,' Jake said, a few moments later when they had all reined to a halt in front of him. 'I reckon somebody must have told you about the jaspers kidnapping the girl.'

Sheriff Slim Parfitt turned his head and very deliberately spat at a boulder. 'Kidnappers, you say?' He looked at the others and laughed.

To Jake's consternation the others, except for the irritatingly impassive Nantan, whom he intended having words with, all burst out laughing.

'Oh we are an official posse, right enough,' said the sheriff 'But we ain't after any kidnappers.' He nodded nonchalantly to the others. 'No sir. We are after a murdering dog, called Scudder!'

Jake was taken entirely by surprise. Before he realized it, he was covered by five guns.

'Shuck your weapons or die in the saddle!' barked the sheriff. And as Jake tossed his gun and his Winchester to the ground the sheriff urged his horse close and suddenly lashed out with his gun, catching Jake a raking blow across the face. 'And that's just something for resisting arrest.'

Jake shook his head and dabbed his broken lip with the back of his hand. 'What are you talking about? Arrest for what?'

'For the murder of that little saloon-girl that I saw you with last night. An ugly mess you made of her with her own scissors.'

'Let's string him up now, Sheriff,' said Deputy Hank Bott.

'Or how about we shoot him here like a dog?' suggested a barrel-chested man with a straggly moustache.

A tall lanky man in an ill-fitting Stetson produced a whiskey-bottle from his saddle-bag. He uncorked it, took a swig then handed it to his neighbour. 'Or there again we could set him loose and have some sport.'

His neighbour a man with dirty corn hair and a patch over one eye grunted. 'Good idea. What say we give him ten minutes start?'

Jake said nothing, realizing that anything he did say would only inflame the situation and probably lead to his death all the sooner. He needed to stay alive, and that meant that he needed to stay quiet and think.

Sheriff Parfitt nodded and took the whiskey bottle. 'The idea has merit, Brooster. I reckon I could do with a coffee, so we could give him as long as that. Then we either shoot him or string him up, depending on whether or not we find a tree or cactus handy.'

'Haven't you forgotten something, Sheriff?' Jake asked as the lawman slaked his whiskey thirst. 'I haven't been formally arrested, far less had a trial of any sort. And I assure you that I haven't killed anyone — especially not a woman.'

Sheriff Parfitt's hand tightened on his

gun. 'You are a liar, Scudder. I saw that poor girl's body. We are all the trial you are gonna get, you murdering dog.'

Nantan had moved between the sheriff and his deputy. He tugged the sheriff's sleeve then leaned over and whispered in his ear. After a moment the sheriff roared with laughter as he clapped the young Apache on the back. 'Damn! Nantan, you have more uses than a whole cathouse of women. You get going and we'll see to this feller.'

As Nantan dismounted and then disappeared up into the rocks the sheriff gestured with his gun for Jake to dismount. Then he reached into his saddlebag and drew out a short shovel, which he tossed at Jake's feet.

'Pick it up, Scudder and start walking. You are going to have some digging to do.'

8

Carmen de Menendez despised Sheriff Slim Parfitt, just as she actually despised most men. Yet she knew that he lusted after her and would damned well sell his soul if she so much as hinted that he might one day share her bed. It was, of course, an idea that repelled her, but as long as he was useful to her she was willing to play the game and string him along.

The screaming show that she put on when she 'found' poor little Rosalind's body was, she felt, a masterstroke. Half of the wasters in town witnessed it, and she massaged the fool of a sheriff's self-esteem so much that he got deputy Hank Bott to whip up three of the most immoral bar-dogs in town to form a posse.

They assembled at the bar of the Busted Flush saloon.

'Why don't you take Nantan?' she

suggested, tremulously, as if the shock of finding Rosalind had shaken her to the core. 'He is a good tracker.'

Slim Parfitt accepted the suggestion with alacrity. 'That was my very thought,' he said, taking one last swig of his complimentary whiskey-bottle, one of those that Carmen de Menendez had instructed Manolito, her head bar-keeper to give to each member of the posse. 'He will run that murdering *hombre* down in no time.'

Carmen de Menendez watched the posse ride off, then quickly went to her private rooms, making it clear that she was going to rest and did not want to be disturbed for the rest of the day. Then she sent Leticia, her personal maid, to go and bring her horse from the livery. Then, while Manolito arranged for drinks on the house, she slipped out of the back of the saloon. She slung her saddle-bags on the bay and slid a well-oiled Winchester into the boot.

Carmen de Menendez was a well-armed and capable woman who was not prepared to let anyone get in the way of her ambition or her destiny.

★ ★ ★

Rubal Cage had left his horse ground-tethered on the other side of the rise from the Rocking H ranch house, then once darkness had fallen he made his way to the bunkhouse. Knowing as he did that it would be empty he had settled down to a peaceful sleep in Bill Coburn's superior bed in the ramrod's room.

At cock-crow he made his way across the yard to the ranch house, about whose geography he had a vague recollection. He let himself in by one of the downstairs windows that had been left open overnight to let in some fresh air. Once inside he grinned to himself as he realized that he had hit the jackpot on his first attempt.

Johnnie Parker was slumbering peacefully in the big brass bed. Rubal Cage crossed the room and drew out his Colt .45. He pressed the barrel against Johnnie's temple as he simultaneously clamped his hand over his mouth.

'Not a sound, Parker!' he whispered between grated teeth. 'You surprised me by still being alive, but so help me I will finish the job I started the other day if you so much as squeak.' Then when Johnnie made a slight nodding movement of his head to indicate his acquiescence, he asked, 'Just how come you are still here? When I shoot a man I expect him to die.'

Johnnie eyed him disdainfully. 'Maybe I wasn't ready to die, Cage. And maybe I will live to see you hang, you miserable — '

Rubal Cage clamped his hand over Johnnie's mouth again and pressed the gun nozzle harder against his temple. 'I'll give you one chance, Parker. Keep quiet until I say so, or you go to meet your maker right now.'

Once again Johnnie nodded, then watched as Cage silently stepped across the room and positioned himself on the other side of the door, as if he had heard a step outside.

A split second later the door burst open and Yucatan stepped in with a handgun in his right fist. 'Mister Johnnie, are you — '

He never finished the sentence as the butt of Rubal Cage's gun thumped down on the back of his neck and the big man went sprawling face down on the floor.

Rubal Cage prodded him with his foot. 'Didn't you ever learn to knock before you come in a room?' he said with a sarcastic laugh. 'Because that is what you can expect from me if you don't.' He picked up Yucatan's gun before Johnnie Parker could even think of getting out of bed.

'Now how about we have a little word with the man of the ranch-house,' he said with a malevolent grin.

*   *   *

Scudder had half-expected to feel the fatal thud of a bullet in his back as he laboured to dig the hole with the small shovel. He was a strong, muscular man at the peak of fitness, yet his breathing was becoming laboured in the heat of the midday sun as he stood in the hole that was now the depth of his shoulders.

'Don't stop yet!' ordered Sheriff Parfitt. 'You ain't hit water yet!'

The other members of the posse went into hysterics at this and another whiskey-bottle did the rounds.

'How deep a grave do you plan on me digging?' Jake asked.

'A grave?' Sheriff Parfitt repeated with mock surprise. 'What makes you think you are digging a grave?'

Jake raised an eyebrow but said nothing, which provoked another out-pouring of laughter from the posse members.

The sheriff suddenly let out a gasp as Nantan silently appeared, as if from nowhere and held out a sack.

'Damn it, Nantan, why do you have to sneak up like that?' Sheriff Parfitt barked, holding his hand up for Nantan to keep the sack. 'And no, I don't need to see it yet.' Then turning to Jake he snarled:

'Toss that shovel out here and put your hands behind your back.'

Jake obeyed and felt someone tie his hands behind him. Then he watched as the barrel-chested man with the straggly moustache picked the shovel up upon a gesture from the sheriff and began piling the sand into the hole around Jake.

'I thought you said this wasn't a grave, Sheriff,' Jake said sarcastically.

'It isn't a grave unless you want it to be,' returned Parfitt with a sly grin.

Ten minutes later only Jake Scudder's head remained above the surface, which had been tamped down by the other posse members.

'OK, Nantan,' said the sheriff. 'Time to show the man his new friend.'

Jake watched in horror as the young Apache opened his sack and held it steadily for a moment before darting a hand inside and catching hold of something. A moment later he withdrew his hand, which was clutching the unmistakable wriggling body of a diamondback rattlesnake.

Jake was all too aware of the film of perspiration that had developed over his brow and the thump of his rapidly beating heart. He watched in horror as Nantan held it behind its flat, triangular head and dexterously tied a loop of rope about its tail, just above its rattle. Then he signalled to Deputy Bott, who tied the other end of the rope to a wooden stake that he had already hammered into the ground about six feet away.

And then Nantan slowly lowered the snake to the ground, stretching its rope to its full extent.

'You devil!' Jake gasped, straining his head back as far as he could. He was all too aware that the distance of the stake from his head had been carefully gauged. At full stretch the rattler would be able to reach within a couple of inches of his face. If he relaxed he faced a painful death.

Sheriff Parfitt and the posse positively dissolved into hysterics at the sight of the angry snake and the clearly petrified Jake Scudder.

'Hope you have a strong neck, Scudder,' laughed the sheriff. 'Because that is what you would have needed if we had just hanged you. At least this way you've got a chance — if you can outlast the rattler!'

Hank Bott, the deputy, grinned. 'Of course, in this heat you are both going to get mighty dry without water or shade.'

Jake was too engrossed with simple survival to reply. That the reptile was full of hate and anger was all too obvious.

'Must say it is getting hot,' Sheriff Parfitt said, removing his hat and wiping his brow with the back of his hand. 'You might think about all the discomfort you are causing us, Scudder,' he said accusingly.

The impassive Nantan tugged the sheriff's sleeve and whispered in his ear. The sheriff grinned and nodded. 'Reckon that makes sense, Nantan,' he said. 'Coffee and chow sounds a good idea. We will give the bastard a bit of time with his executioner, and then we will be back. No sense in us all burning in this heat.'

He knelt beside Jake's head and grinned. 'And in case the snake doesn't get you, just remember that I've got six bullets in this Peacemaker of mine — and any one of them will be enough to put you out of your misery if you just care to holler.'

★   ★   ★

Elly had not felt like eating the rancid bacon nor drink the thick black Arbuckle's coffee that the two men gave her. However, she was all too aware that she would need her strength and her wits about her come what might. They had locked her in the dark, windowless back room of a cabin in the Pintos, which she had little doubt would be almost impossible to find. A solitary guttering candle was her only illumination.

The fact that the men made no attempt to cover their faces alarmed her no end. Even more disconcerting, they didn't even bother to conceal their names from her. And indeed, she was almost sure that one of them had worked for her father for a while, until he had fired him.

'Damn it, Hog,' she heard the younger one, the coarse-featured one with a lazy eye, say as he closed and bolted the door behind him, 'she's a looker. Why for two pins — '

'For two pins you will keep your trap shut,' said the other, the one Elly noticed had a badly bandaged ear. 'We are here to do a job, that's all. You know what Rubal said — keep our eyes peeled and be ready to shoot.'

Elly had been about to take another sip of her coffee, but stopped with the tin mug half-way to her lips when she heard the name.

Cage? Rubal Cage? She was sure that she had heard that name several times before. Then she remembered. He had been the ramrod of the Double J, she was sure. And Jeb Jackson had fired him because of some trouble with the way he looked after the horses and critters. And there were other, darker rumours, which made her spine shiver.

What do they want of me? she thought, once again trying to puzzle out the whole situation. It seemed clear that these men had been involved in the rustling, no doubt with others who had probably been paid off after the herd had been sold to the C & SW Cattle Company. And so where did Rubal Cage fit in? Were they planning to hold her to ransom in the mistaken belief that Saul would be able to raise any money at all?

A thought struck her and she willed herself to chew on the bacon. Perhaps Rubal Cage's dismissal had all been a ploy. What if he was still working for Jeb Jackson, albeit clandestinely?

Questions! Just questions and suppositions, she thought with a frown. And in part that frown was aimed at Jake Scudder, the man who had said so confidently that he was going to look after her. Well where was he? She swallowed the bacon and took a hefty gulp of the strong black coffee.

Whoring, that was where! she concluded. Probably still loitering about in bed with one of the girls from the Busted Flush saloon! At the very thought she pushed the plate aside and grasped the spoon — the only utensil they had given her. 'You are on your own, Elly Horrocks,' she whispered to herself 'Fine! That means you have to get yourself out of this prison before those devils out there come in and try to rape you, or — or worse!'

She got up and surveyed the interior of the room with its dirt floor. As quietly as she could she went and tested each of the wooden slats that made up the walls. To her chagrin she realized that none of them was loose or weak anywhere. And that meant that her only way out was going to be through the floor.

She drew a deep breath, pulling her stomach in as far as she could, as she tried to assess how deep she was going to have to burrow.

'No time to waste, then,' she mused. And settling down on her knees she began to dig the dirt floor by the far wall with her spoon.

★　★　★

The sun had long reached its zenith and Jake felt the exposed skin on his neck and face begin to burn, was sure that in some parts blisters were beginning to rise.

From a distance away he heard the ever more raucous banter of the posse as they cooked a meal and drank more whiskey. Despite his predicament, how-ever, such was his approach to life and all that it could throw at him that he would not allow himself to permit the thought of defeat or despair. There was no way that he would give up in his struggle to survive, and give the sadistic sheriff the pleasure of seeing him beg for a bullet in the brain.

'I just wish I had a hat,' he mumbled to himself. Then, perhaps partly from semi-delirium as he lost body fluid and partly from his steely personality, he found himself grinning at the thought of his head with a Stetson sticking out of the sand, with a rattler trying to give him a kiss on the nose.

As he thought it the flat head made a lunge at him, as if divining his thought.

'You sure are an angry varmint, aren't you?' he asked the snake. 'I don't suppose there would be much use me trying to sing to you or whistle a bit. I can't see that would calm you down any.'

But as he looked into the snake's eyes it seemed that all he could see was hate. As if it was determined to kill this creature who was sharing its captivity and its experience of the baking early afternoon sun.

Jake's neck was aching almost beyond endurance as he strove to keep himself as far from the snake as possible. Indeed, so focused upon the rattlesnake was he, its head mere inches from his own, that he failed to hear the approach of another.

A hand suddenly clamped itself over his face, pulling his head back at such an angle that he feared for a moment that his neck would snap. Then he saw another hand appear with the long double-edged blade of a hunting knife. It glistened in the sun.

He realized that his throat was now maximally exposed. He shut his eyes and gritted his teeth as he waited to feel the blade flash across to slit his throat.

9

Elly had been listening to the two men with half an ear, aware that their voices had been getting progressively both louder and more slurred. Her main focus of attention, however, had been on the slowly widening hole that she had managed to scoop out. After an hour she had managed to reach the lower edge of the wooden slats that formed the back wall of the cabin. Working with the spoon and her hands she had then managed to enlarge it enough to the point where she thought she might be able to just squeeze through. But that meant creating a hole big enough on the other side so that she could literally burrow under.

One of the men had started singing the most offensive ribald songs and she began to fear that at any moment the door would be unbolted and one or both of them would enter to have their way with her.

But at last she felt she had made enough room to try wriggling through. Her first attempt, however, made her realize that she had underestimated and she had to work on the hole again. Her hands by then were filthy, blistered and bleeding, but she could not afford to stop. On her second attempt she managed to wriggle under the slats, twisting herself round as she did so, so that she blinked repeatedly as the overhead sun seared her eyes.

As she was struggling to get her waist under the slats she heard a metallic ratcheting noise followed by a click, as the hammer of a handgun was pulled back.

'Can I give you a hand, lady?' guffawed Cole Lancing. Then as Elly gasped and craned her neck back to see him, he called out:

'You can cut the caterwauling now, Hog. Your little joke worked a treat,' He grinned at her, his teeth yellowed with

157

tobacco. 'I reckon that little bit of exercise will have tired you out, lady. Nicely tired!'

★   ★   ★

All Jake could feel was pain in the neck as his head was pulled back. Then he heard a sickening noise as the knife cut through flesh and bone and his face was splattered with blood.

Then slowly the hand over his face eased and he opened his eyes to see the diamondback's bloody head mere inches from him, its sightless eyes staring straight at him, a hunting-knife skewering its skull to the ground.

'Keep quiet when I take my hand away,' a voice whispered in his ear. 'Then I will get you out of there.'

Jake nodded, tried to speak, then felt his head slump forwards in a faint.

How long he was unconscious he did not know. When he did regain consciousness he had been dug free, hauled out and laid on top of the ground several feet away from the grisly body of the rattlesnake. He noted that the hunting-knife had been removed.

'Drink this,' came the voice again. 'Then we must be swift. The sheriff and his men will come soon.'

Jake drank lukewarm water from the canteen and then rubbed his weary eyes as he tried to focus on his saviour. Eventually, in disbelief, he gasped:

'Nantan!'

'It is I. I am sorry that I had to put you through this trial with the snake, but it was the only way I could think to keep you alive.'

'And I thought that you drugged our brandy. I thought — '

'That I was one of them?' The young man shook his head. 'I did not know that the brandy I brought you was poisoned.'

Jake's features clouded. 'And what about Rosalind? Is it true? Is she dead?'

'I am afraid so. She was a good girl and did not deserve to die. I have vowed that her death will be avenged. I knew that you had nothing to do with her death.' His face suddenly registered deep emotion. 'And that is two vows I have made. The first is to kill the dog who raped my sister.'

And fleetingly Nantan told Jake of the day a man came to their camp, beat Nantan up and left him for dead. But when he regained consciousness he found his sister's body defiled and brutally bludgeoned to death.

'He was of my people,' he went on. 'An animal that must be put down.' He bent his head and parted his long hair at the back to show an ugly scar where he had been pistol-whipped. 'I tracked him to Silver City several moons ago, but he had disappeared. I have an idea that he will return, which is why I have stayed and done whatever work people will pay me for.'

'Including at the Busted Flush saloon?'

'Yes, and whenever people need a guide for hunting. Or when the sheriff needs a tracker.'

'Do you know anything about Miss Horrocks?'

'I heard that you were tracking her and the men who kidnapped her. I have seen their tracks. Three horses and a cowpony. The trail leads here and then goes to the west.'

'That was what I thought,' said Jake. 'I had better get after them.'

Nantan nodded and pointed to a patch of scruboak where he had tethered Jake's stallion and his palomino. 'The sheriff and his men are almost on the point of madness with their fire-water. I will take your stallion and lead them away, while you wait here until they have gone.'

Jake stood up, maintaining his balance with some difficulty. 'Where will you lead them, Nantan?'

The ghost of a smile played across Nantan's lips. 'I already took your hat. It will add to the impression that I am you. I can circle round and round in these mountains for days if needs be. Then I will take them to Tucksville.' He handed Jake his gun and holster, then mounted the stallion. 'Wait until I have drawn them away, Scudder, then get after those men. Do not let them do anything to that lady.'

As he rode off at a gallop in the direction of the posse's temporary camp he let off a couple of shots. Then he headed off towards Rattlesnake Pass. There were shouts of consternation, much swearing, followed soon after by the noise of horses charging after Nantan, and the discharging of weapons.

'You are a good kid, Nantan,' Jake said, mounting the palomino and picking up the tracks again. 'Let's hope that we can both avenge that little Rosalind!'

★   ★   ★

Elly had found herself unceremoniously dragged out of her escape hole and pushed roughly back into the cabin.

'We got ourselves a regular gopher,'

sneered Cole Lancing. 'What you think we should do with her, Hog?'

'Tie her up and let her kick her heels, I reckon. A few hours without food and water should sort her out.'

And so Elly found herself back in the darkened room she thought that she had escaped from just a short while before. This time, however, she was tied hand and foot and then tied down to the crude bunk. A thousand curses had formed in her mind as Cole Lancing tied her, but she bit her tongue and was quiet. She realized that reprisals, or worse, could come swiftly from men such as these. So once she was alone she just lay listening to their foul-mouthed banter and raucous singing as she tried to think of a way of freeing herself. Every few minutes she heaved at her bonds in an attempt to gradually loosen them. But it seemed in vain.

What time it was she had no way of knowing, except that the solitary entrance of light from the hole she had made was beginning to darken.

Then suddenly, she almost cried out in alarm when she saw a long shape emerge from the hole.

A snake! she imagined.

And then as she focused on it properly she realized that it was a human arm.

'Scudder?' she whispered.

'It's me, Elly,' his voice whispered back. 'You OK?'

Elly gave a deep sigh. 'I have been better. But I can't move, Jake. I am all tied up.'

'How many of them are there? Two or three?'

'Two. The third one is called Rubal Cage. He went on somewhere early this morning.'

'Stay where you are!' he said.

Elly bit back the retort that had formed on her tongue, saying instead: 'Be careful, Jake.'

In the main cabin Hog Fleming and Cole Lancing were playing cards at a plain deal table, the remains of a meal before them and the dregs of a whiskey-bottle in the middle of the table.

'I reckon you are going to have to pay me all of your share from the herd when you see my hand,' said Lancing, his lazy eye looking positively alert for a moment.

Hog Fleming snorted. 'Or maybe it will be you that pays me, you piece of misery.' He tapped the table. 'I want to see what's in your hand.'

So engrossed with their card-game were they that neither of them had heard the door being silently pushed open.

'Maybe you had better take a look at what's in my hand!' Jake Scudder snapped.

The two rustlers spun round, amazement written across their faces. Then they both made moves towards their guns.

'I wouldn't if I were you,' said Jake, ratcheting back the hammer of his Remington. 'Now slowly lift those guns and toss them over here.'

Gingerly, the two men lifted their weapons.

Jake's eyes narrowed as they fell on the bloodstained bandage about Hog Fleming's ear. 'You are the dog who shoots unarmed men, aren't you?' He gave a humourless smile. 'It was me that notched your ear.'

Cole Lancing tossed his gun over, then looked nervously at his partner. 'Let him have your gun, Hog,' he urged.

But Hog Fleming's expression had changed from one of surprise to one of ire. 'You did this to me? You bastard! Another dog shot a piece out of my ear before you — and I killed him.'

Jake nodded his head with mock sympathy. 'It must hurt.'

'Damn you! Go to — !' Fleming began, deftly swinging his gun into shooting position.

He was still raising it when a bullet smashed into his forehead, throwing him backwards to fall a lifeless heap against the wall, a rapidly expanding pool of blood from the back of his head seeping into the dirt floor.

'A lot of trouble might have been saved if I had shot him there in the first place, instead of three inches wide,' Jake said coldly. 'Still, it will save the hangman a job.'

Cole Lancing was shaking. 'Hangman? Easy now, mister. There is no harm done. We can come to some arrangement, can't we?'

'Sure we can,' replied Jake. 'But first thing I want you to get into that room and untie Miss Horrocks.'

Lancing nodded firmly and got to his feet. As he did so he noticed that Scudder was swaying slightly on his feet, and that his face looked badly sunburned. He opened the door and led the way inside.

'The ropes are tight,' he said. 'I'll need to cut her free.'

'Are you OK, Elly,' Jake asked. 'They haven't harmed you?'

'Not yet. Only my pride.'

Jake nodded for the rustler to begin

freeing her. He watched as the rustler opened a clasp knife and cut the bonds about her feet and the ones which lashed her to the bunk.

Lancing was reaching for the ones at her wrists when he noted the look of concern on Elly's face.

'Jake, are you . . . ?'

In the corner of his eye Cole Lancing had seen Jake sway again. He took his chance and hit out backwards with his elbow, catching Jake in the stomach. The gun in Jake's hand went off, drilling a hole in the wall. Instantly, Lancing, who had faced many a knife-fight in his time wheeled round, his hand rising and falling to slash across Jake's forearm. Jake cried out in pain, the gun falling from his hand.

'Not so tough now, are you, big man!' growled Lancing, dexterously reversing the knife and preparing to lunge at Jake's chest.

But Elly had sprung up. Swinging her bound hands she caught the rustler behind the knees, causing them to buckle.

It gave Jake the opportunity he needed to recover. He drilled a straight left into Lancing's face, breaking his nose and propelling him backwards to smash into the wall. He slowly slid down to lie in an unconscious heap.

'Well done, Elly,' said Jake. 'I am glad that — '

Then before he could finish, his knees began to buckle and he slumped to the ground in a faint.

When he recovered consciousness he found himself lying on the bunk. A piece of flannel soaked in water was pressed to his forehead and Elly was bandaging the knife-slash on his fore-arm.

'What about the other one?' he asked, attempting to rise.

Elly pushed him back. 'You need to rest a while. I don't know exactly what you have been through, but it looks as if you might have seen something of hell. Your face is so sunburned.'

She gestured to the other side of the room, where Cole Lancing was lying, his hands and feet bound and a gag in his mouth. 'I thought I had better get him tied up before he regained consciousness,' she explained. 'Now tell me what happened, Jake.'

And while she brewed coffee, having covered Hog Fleming's body with a blanket, she listened to Jake's account of all that had happened since she left to go with Sheriff Parfitt to see the C & SW Cattle Company agent in Silver City.

Elly covered her mouth in horror. 'They killed that poor girl?'

Jake nodded. 'Someone did. And for that there will be a reckoning!'

'But we still don't know who stole the herd,' Elly said, pouring coffee into two tin mugs. 'Except that Rubal Cage and Hog Fleming were involved. Cage used to work for the Double J ranch and Fleming was fired by my father.'

Jake scowled. 'And that jasper won't talk.' He clicked his tongue as he cast the bound rustler a scathing look. 'Still, I reckon he might talk once the prospect of hanging hits him.'

'Are we taking him with us, Jake?'

'I think we should, except — '

'Except we have not got time on our side. We would have to travel more slowly. Couldn't we just leave him here? Make sure he has water?'

Jake thought for a moment then nodded. 'You are right, Elly. We can't go to Silver City, since the sheriff and his drunken posse are chasing me, so I guess we had better head for Tucksville. And I hope that hidebound constable will listen for once.'

Elly swilled her coffee in her mug. 'Then the sooner we start the better. It is almost dark and I don't think I could stand spending a night here.'

10

It was almost dark by the time Carmen de Menendez reached the cabin. She raised her hand to her mouth and made the prearranged signal whistle. But there was no reply. She cursed under her breath. Unlike Rubal Cage she did not have a high opinion of either Hog Fletcher or Cole Lancing. She knew that for dirty work you had to be prepared to use men with no scruples whatsoever. Almost inevitably, she thought, that meant using men of limited intelligence. Yet for all that, both men had survived a reasonable length of time in the southwest, considering their way of life. It was for that reason that she began to feel uneasy.

She pulled out her Winchester from the boot, dismounted and made her way stealthily towards the cabin.

As she circled it she noted the hole at

the back, which set her mind working. Could the girl have escaped? Could that be it? Were those two fools at that moment chasing her somewhere in the Pintos?

She gingerly undid the latch of the door and pushed it open. By the failing light she could see a blanket covering a bundle against the wall on the far side of the table, which was strewn with cards, dirty dishes and an almost empty bottle of whiskey.

'Hog? Cole?' she ventured.

From the room at the back she fancied that she heard movement. 'Are you in there?'

She crossed the room and prodded the door open with the barrel of her Winchester.

Cole Lancing was frantically kicking his feet against the dirt floor and shaking his head back and forth.

Carmen de Menendez tore the gag from his mouth. 'What the hell have you two done?' she demanded angrily. 'Where is the girl and where is Hog?'

'Hog is in there and he is stone dead! And the girl has gone. That Scudder guy came and jumped us.' His lip curled maliciously. 'I managed to cut him up a little, though.'

If he had expected a reward, it was not the one he received. She gave him a backhanded swipe across the face. 'You fool! You could have ruined everything.'

She produced a knife, leaned her Winchester against the wall and cut him free. 'Now show me Hog,' she ordered.

Cole Lancing heaved himself up, rubbing his wrists to restore circulation. He went back through to the main room, and lifted the blanket to show the stiffened corpse of the rustler. 'I will kill that Scudder for you, Hog,' he said.

And then to the saloon-owner: 'Should I bury him?'

'No time,' she snapped. 'We have to get going.'

★ ★ ★

Sheriff Slim Parfitt was madder than a rattlesnake with its tail tied to a stake. At least that was how he felt after several hours spent chasing Scudder's stallion in and out of canyons around Rattlesnake Pass.

'When we catch that bastard, there will be no more fooling around with snakes,' he snarled at Hank Bott, his deputy and the other three members of the posse. He remounted his horse, having inspected the ground for fresh tracks. 'It will be a straight bullet through the brain for all this aggravation he's caused.'

'What do you make of that Nantan, Sheriff?' asked the deputy.

'Damned if I know where he's gone, but if he's just headed back to Silver City, I will root him out and — '

'Give him his own rattlesnake treatment?' Sly Ryker, the tall rider with an ill-fitting Stetson asked hopefully.

'Maybe,' replied the sheriff, signalling for them all to follow him. 'But first let's concentrate on finding Scudder.

Then we'll settle with Nantan. Come on, he went this way.'

As they trotted after the sheriff in the failing light, Nantan gave a silent grunt of satisfaction from his viewpoint above. He was pleased with the false trail he had set them. He yawned and made himself comfortable, sure in the knowledge that they would be at least an hour getting back to this point. And that would be quite enough time for him to have a refreshing sleep, before he set another false trail.

* * *

Jake and Elly were riding along one of the canyons that ran parallel to Rattlesnake Pass in the last stage of evening before darkness fell. Although the moon was doing its best to illuminate the country, the canyon was so deep and narrow that little moonlight ever hit the bottom. Accordingly, it was slow going.

'Are you sure we are going the right way, Jake?'

Jake half-turned. 'Pretty sure. One thing I seem to have been blessed with is a good sense of direction. And pretty soon we'll have a few stars to help us along. I reckon we follow this for a couple of miles then we should come out close to the mouth of the pass.

'But do you — ?'

He hissed and raised his hand to indicate silence. 'I thought I heard something,' he whispered.

Then a moment later they heard the unmistakeable sound of several horses riding close by.

'My God! Who is it?' Elly whispered.

'Can't be sure, but I reckon it must be Sheriff Parfitt and his posse,' replied Jake. 'Sound travels in strange ways in these canyons. They could be some way off, or — they could be round the next bend.'

'Wh . . . what should we do?'

'Only one safe thing to do. We had better bed down for the night and hope that they pass and keep on going. In the morning we can start afresh.'

* * *

Carmen de Menendez was a hell-cat! The most beautiful hell-cat in the world, but not a woman to cross. At least that was Cole Lancing's assessment. It wasn't that he felt particularly close to Hog Fleming, but he felt bad about just leaving him to rot in that cabin, a prey to coyotes and all the other creatures of the night that would home in on the smell of death and fresh meat. He cringed at the thought.

'How come you came here by yourself, Miss Carmen?' he ventured as they rode quickly through the darkness, making good time.

'I came to make sure that Rubal Cage and you two didn't screw up,' she replied, eyeing his silhouette with displeasure. 'And it looks as if I was certainly right to do so!'

Lancing had a thick hide and the sarcasm was lost on him. 'But how come that Scudder managed to get after us? I thought the plan was for him to get taken care of in town.'

'You mean like the way he saw you and Hog off?'

Cole stiffened as the import of that remark stung. 'He was lucky, Miss Carmen. No, I thought that something else was planned. That is what Rubal said, but he's a bit like his name — 'cagy'! He began to laugh at his own wit, but was silenced by a flick of her quirt on his exposed hand.

'Don't ask so many questions, Cole!'

He rubbed his hand. 'Sorry, Miss Carmen. It is just that — you know — with Hog gone, there's got to be more money coming my way — right? The thing is, I kind of took a fancy to that little girl that we were supposed to separate from Scudder. With some money, maybe I could buy . . . '

Carmen de Menendez slowed down and turned to Cole. In the moonlight he could see her shining white teeth and realized that she was smiling at him. Men did strange things when Carmen de Menendez smiled at them, as Cole Lancing well knew.

'You have been a good man through all of this, Cole,' she purred. 'And you have taken a fancy to little Rosalind, have you? Well don't you worry. As soon as we get back to Silver City when this is all over, I will have a word with her. That bonus that is coming your way could set the pair of you up.' She reached over and squeezed his wrist. 'Trust me. I will take care of you, Cole.'

As they set off again, Cole Lancing rode with a light heart. He was riding with a beautiful woman in the moonlight — a hell-cat, admittedly — but he was on her good side. And she was going to take care of him. He felt good about it.

★   ★   ★

Hangover headache and stomach pains from lack of breakfast did nothing to ease the temper of Sheriff Slim Parfitt's posse the following morning.

'I reckon that Scudder is playing with

you, Sheriff,' said Hank Bott.

'Yeah, he's leading us in circles,' agreed Sly Ryker.

'More like figures of eight,' moaned Tod Latimer, the barrel-chested local blacksmith who was beginning to miss his forge more than usual.

'Why don't we split up then?' suggested Wade Carson, adjusting his eye-patch. 'That way we could catch him when he loops back on himself.'

Sheriff Parfitt took a slug of whiskey, his favoured remedy for early morning hangover relief. He sucked air between his teeth as the fiery liquid hit his stomach and he immediately felt in control of himself and of the situation.

'Pipe down all of you. I am the sheriff of Silver City and I am in charge. I know exactly what that murdering dog Scudder is up to and I guarantee we will have him by the end of today. Now saddle up and get ready to follow me, as soon as I pick up the trail again.'

And indeed, it did not take Slim Parfitt long to find the trail, for Nantan had made it as obvious as humanly possible. Once again he was watching them from a vantage point high up in the rocks, sure in his mind that they would eventually find their way up to where he now lay, and thence along the snaking route that he planned to take right into Tucksville.

★ ★ ★

Elly and Jake had settled down for the night and waited for the riders to move away, which they surely had. Then with first light, after a breakfast of cold beans and water they saddled up and continued on their way towards Tucksville.

Until they heard the echoing of horses on the move.

'I rather think that is the posse again,' said Jake. 'It may be that they are following Nantan all the way to Tucksville. I had hoped that he would lose them in the Pintos.'

'So will it be too dangerous to go to

Tucksville?' Elly queried. 'But couldn't I go? There's no reason for them to stop me.'

'Except we don't know whether they have any knowledge about the killing. They could be in on this whole thing, or they could just be stooges that are being used by whoever is behind all this.'

'Then I think the best bet is to go to the Double J and get Jeb Jackson to help us.'

Jake shook his head doubtfully. 'I am not so sure, Elly. Maybe it would be better if we start by getting you back safely to the ranch. I am betting that your brother must be frantic by now.' He smiled, and then added:

'To say nothing of that young man of yours.'

* * *

Johnnie Parker was more anxious than he thought was possible. But having lost so much blood and with his wounds only half-healed he felt well nigh helpless. Rubal Cage had gagged and tied him hand and foot, then left him on the bed while he dragged the unconscious Yucatan 'through the ranch-house hall to surprise Saul Horrocks.

From time to time Johnnie heard Saul's raised voice as he argued and pleaded with Rubal Cage.

'You just sit tight, Horrocks,' he heard Cage say. 'We are all just going to have a nice wait.'

'What for?' Saul Horrocks had demanded.

'Never you mind. You three men are just going to have to enjoy my cooking. Those ropes aren't too uncomfortable are they?' And then he laughed and humiliated each one of them in turn.

True to his word he had fed and watered them, even allowed individual toilet relief, under his scrutiny with his Colt .45.

And so it had gone on through a whole day and night until in the morning Johnnie spied two riders approaching the ranch. A man and a woman.

*　*　*

Nantan was enjoying himself. A natural horseman, he had quickly bonded with the big black stallion and revelled in the ease with which he had led and misled the posse.

He now ambled into Tucksville and made his way along the main street to the nearest saloon. He hitched the stallion outside, then crossed to the other side of the street, selected a spot on the boardwalk and sat down with his back to the wall of a hardware store. Knocking Scudder's Stetson out of shape, Apache style, he pulled it low to cover his face.

He looked just like any number of loafers who could be found doing nothing in a town like Tucksville.

*　*　*

Elly and Jake hitched their horses outside the Rocking H ranch-house, sadly looking so deserted in comparison to the busy place it had been but a few days before.

Elly mounted the steps to the door and pushed it open.

'Saul! Johnnie! It's me. I am back.'

The main room door opened and Carmen de Menendez came out, a broad welcoming smile on her beautiful face. 'Elly, my dear,' she said.

Elly stared at her in amazement, unable to find words. But Jake Scudder, entering a couple of paces behind her managed to find something to say.

'Miss Carmen? What on earth are you doing here?'

Then he felt the unmistakable prod of a gun nozzle being shoved into his back. It was followed by a snarling voice. 'Remember me, Scudder?'

As Jake turned his head he caught a fleeting glimpse of Cole Lancing's lazy eye staring at him. Then there was a blur of movement and excruciating pain as the gun crashed on the back of his head and he went down, pole-axed.

Elly stared in disbelief, then she gasped:

'Saul? Johnnie? Yucatan? Where . . . ?'

Carmen de Menendez was still smiling. 'That is just what I was about to tell you, my dear. They are all in here,' she said, stepping aside for Elly to enter the room. 'We've all been waiting for you.'

11

Sheriff Parfitt and his posse rode into Tucksville amid a cloud of dust. The usual crowd of loafers and urchins quickly congregated in their wake and followed them up the main street.

'There's the stallion,' said Slim Parfitt, turning to give Hank Bott a smug grin. 'I told you all that I would run him down. Now we will get the dog.'

'But where is he?' Sly Ryker queried, looking up and down the street, without seeing the man they knew as Scudder.

Sheriff Parfitt gave him a slap with his hat, showering him with an accumulation of trail dust. 'You expecting him to be sauntering around?' he asked sarcastically.

'Why not?' rebutted Ryker. 'I guess he thinks he gave us the slip a long time ago.'

'Yeah,' agreed Tod Latimer. 'He probably thinks we gave up and headed back to Silver City.'

Slim Parfitt dismounted beside the stallion and gave it a quick examination. 'It's been here a while, anyway. This horse is all cooled down.' He hitched his gunbelt a little higher and pointed his chin at the saloon. 'We'll check in there first. Follow me and all of you spread out as soon as we get inside.'

It was dark inside after the brightness of the morning sun. A solitary bartender was unstacking chairs in readiness for the start of the day's trading.

'I am afraid that we are not open yet, gents,' he said.

'Well, I reckon you will open for us,' said Slim Parfitt, wiping the back of his hand across his parched lips. 'Make it whiskey for five.'

The bartender was a tall, thin man with a long nose and defiant eyes. 'I reckon not. It isn't allowed in Tucksville for another half-hour.'

Slim Parfitt tapped his star. 'Don't you see who I am?' he said pompously. 'I am Sheriff Slim Parfitt of Silver City and I am in charge of this posse here.'

'Still no whiskey,' returned the bartender. 'Isn't that right, Deputy McCaid?'

All five turned as a small, tubby man of about fifty with pebble-thick wire-framed spectacles stepped through the batwing doors. The posse members looked disdainfully at the slightly comic figure standing before them in a shirt buttoned up to the collar and with a crudely made deputy constable badge pinned to a waistcoat which strained over his paunch.

'That is certainly correct, Amos. No drinking at this time of the day. Constable Matt Brooks won't countenance it at all.'

'The hell with that!' exclaimed Sheriff Parfitt. 'Now you just look here, Deputy whatever-your-name is, I am the sheriff of Silver City and I am aiming to take a murdering dog by the name of Jake Scudder into custody.'

'Do you know that he is in Tucksville?' Deputy McCaid asked, peering myopically from one to another of the posse.

'That is his black stallion hitched out there.'

'This Jake Scudder. Is he a young Apache kid?'

Slow understanding crept across Parfitt's face, which coloured rapidly with ire. 'Nantan! He has been playing games with us! I'll kill him! Come on, men.'

And as one they all rushed past the deputy into the street.

Nantan was now leaning against a post on the opposite boardwalk, smiling at them.

'Nantan! You damned well suckered us,' snarled Slim Parfitt. 'Well, we are going to teach you a lesson you will never forget. Get him, boys.'

Another voice entered the affray. 'Hold it right there. You and your men will teach nobody anything in this town, Slim Parfitt. And don't even think of going for your guns. Any of you.'

All five of the posse swivelled round to see the tall capable-looking figure of Constable Matt Brooks. He was standing with his feet apart and with his hands hanging casually by his sides.

'Constable Brooks,' hissed Slim Parfitt. 'I know you and you know me. I am the sheriff of Silver City and I have reason to believe that that Nantan feller there has been obstructing me in the execution of my duty. He has helped a known murderer escape my posse. I am therefore taking him in.'

Matt Brooks shook his head. 'And I repeat — not in my town. You have no jurisdiction here.'

A large crowd had been gathering on the boardwalks as people slowly emerged from stores and offices to see what all the raised voices were about.

Sheriff Parfitt's face was now puce with rage. 'Do you think you can stop five of us all by yourself, Brooks?'

Deputy Samuel McCaid had circled the group and now stood a few feet away from Matt Brooks.

'There are two of us here, in case you didn't notice. Me and my deputy.'

The five men stared at the middle-aged deputy with the thick-lensed spectacles and all made sneering noises.

'That isn't polite,' said Matt Brooks. Then with a nod to his deputy, he said: 'I reckon these men could do with a little lesson in manners. How about it, Samuel?'

None of the posse was ready for the blur of movement that followed. And the crowd of onlookers would spread the word, so that it grew into a local legend. Such is the way in towns like Tucksville.

Constable Matt Brooks was fast and before anyone could account for it a gun had appeared in his hand. Yet his speed was as nothing compared to his deputy, Samuel McCaid. His blue steel Colt had seemed to jump into his hands and five shots rang out before any of the posse had moved a muscle. With each shot a little cloud of dust rose from between each of the posse members' feet.

Constable Brooks smiled. 'Allow me to introduce my deputy, Samuel McCaid, formerly known as Pebble-eye McCaid the scourge of the badlands.' He raised his gun. 'And like I said, you have no jurisdiction in this town, so I don't take kindly to you throwing your weight around. But threatening a citizen and two of the town's lawmen cannot be allowed.'

'Now you just — ' began Slim Parfitt.

'Quiet there while the constable is talking,' snapped Deputy McCaid.

'Thank you, Samuel,' returned Matt Brooks. Then to the posse: 'All of you shuck your weapons and then make your way over to the town jail. Pebble-eye will look after you.'

As the disarmed posse members filed along the street, Deputy McCaid grinned and whispered to his constable:

'First real-life sheriff I ever locked up. This will be kind of fun.'

Matt Brooks patted him on the arm and grinned as the bemused and amazed crowd followed the deputy and his captives down the street, everyone full of awe and renewed respect for the man they had previously thought of as a joke.

Matt Brooks looked up at the impassive Nantan and gestured for him to join him. 'I guess that you and I ought to have a little chat,' he said.

★　★　★

When Jake Scudder regained consciousness he found that his hands were tied and that he had been dumped unceremoniously in a swivel-chair beside a desk. Elly was sitting beside Johnnie Parker who was lying on a couch, and Saul and the big Yucatan were both sitting with their hands tied in front of them. Saul Horrocks looked exceedingly gaunt and dispirited in his Bath chair.

'So this is the guy who has caused so much trouble,' sneered Rubal Cage, lashing out with his fist and catching Jake across the face.

Jake shook his head to clear his vision. He blinked and found himself looking at three people who were standing with guns in their hands. He recognized Carmen de Menendez and the rustler Cole Lancing.

'And you must be Rubal Cage,' Jake returned, speaking directly to the black-clad man who had struck him. 'I have heard a lot about you. You worked for the neighbouring ranch until you were fired.'

Saul Horrocks interjected, 'He is a treacherous dog. Jeb Jackson recognized his type and threw him out.'

Rubal Cage's lip curled. 'Yes, but look who has the upper hand here — and all the cards. We have the money for your herd, we've got you — and we are about to reel in the most important prize of all.'

Jake nodded his head. 'I guess that means that you expect to get the Double J ranch somehow. Maybe by somehow getting hold of the rancher himself.'

Carmen de Menendez smiled. 'For a murderer you are a clever man, Jake Scudder. And just how did you know this? How did you work it out?'

Jake nodded his head at Elly and Saul. 'Before we left for Silver City I learned all about the ranches around here. It seems that the Double J ranch is the biggest and therefore the wealthiest in this territory. That has to be why you kidnapped Elly — you planned to ransom her, but not to Saul. You planned to ransom her to Jeb Jackson.'

Rubal Cage glanced at Carmen de Menendez and Cole Lancing. 'Will you be OK watching them all while I go and catch the big fish? I will be back in half an hour at the most.'

After he left, they all sat in silence while Carmen de Menendez paced back and forth and Cole Lancing picked his yellowed teeth. The big grandfather clock near the bureau ticked away the seconds. After half an hour or so Carmen de Menendez broke the silence.

'Tell me, Jake Scudder, how did you manage to escape the clutches of our esteemed sheriff of Silver City and his posse?'

Jake gave her a wan smile. 'One word — Nantan.'

The saloon-owner snapped her fingers. 'Ah, I should have known that he was not as trustworthy as I thought.' She looked at Yucatan, who seemed uneasy under her regard. 'It is always a problem with him and his like.'

Saul Horrocks eyed her sourly. 'What sort of a woman are you? Why have you come into our lives?'

Carmen de Menendez laughed, then blew disdainfully through her ruby-red lips. 'And what sort of a life is it that you have, Mr Saul Horrocks? Who are you to question me when you can't even — walk!'

Saul Horrocks' hands trembled with

rage, occasioning further mirth from his captor.

'Miss Carmen,' said Cole Lancing. 'There's a rider coming fast. It looks like Rubal and he's on his own.'

When Rubal Cage appeared through the door a few moments later Carmen de Menendez demanded of him: 'Where is Jackson?'

'He's dead,' Cage replied. 'I shot the bastard.'

Carmen de Menendez did not take her eyes off the others. 'Tell me exactly what happened,' she said calmly.

'The old fool was working in that fancy counting-house study of his, just like I knew he would be at this time of day. He was all alone in the place except for his housekeeper.' He grinned maliciously. 'And she is now an ex-housekeeper.'

'Was Jackson armed?'

'No, not then.'

Carmen de Menendez took a deep breath. 'Go on.'

'I told him that we had the girl and

her brother under armed guard and that he was to empty his safe for me. It is a big one behind a map on the wall. I knew it was there and I knew it would contain a fortune.'

'That was not part of the plan!' the saloon-owner snapped.

Rubal Cage snorted dismissively. 'But it was too good an opportunity to miss. And I hate missing opportunities. What could go wrong, I thought. I had a gun trained on his back all the time.'

Elly glared at Cage in disgust. 'You killed Jeb in cold blood? You monster!'

'Shut up, bitch!' he yelled. 'I didn't kill the fool in cold blood. The bastard pulled out a derringer and slammed the safe closed before I could stop him. He took a shot at me, so I had to kill him.' He spat on the floor as if to indicate an end of the matter.

'You should have just winged him,' said Carmen de Menendez.

'Damn that! He had two barrels on that toy shooter. He could have done me serious harm.'

Carmen de Menendez spoke over her shoulder to Cole Lancing. 'Make sure no one moves.'

Then she turned and shot Rubal Cage in the face. His body was thrown back to smash through the window, where it hung over the ledge.

'He just reached the end of his usefulness,' she said, as if by way of explanation.

The effect on everyone in the room had been of utter shock. Everyone stared aghast at her callousness. Everyone in the room, that was, except Elly and Johnnie Parker.

Slowly throughout the last half-hour Elly had been gradually untying his bound hands. Now she plucked up a cushion and threw it at the woman, before making a dive at her.

'Go, Johnnie! You are our only chance!' she cried.

And while Johnnie Parker dived from the room she closed on Carmen de Menendez, reaching for her gun.

Saul Horrocks stared in wide eyed

alarm. 'No, Elly! She is dangerous!'

Cole Lancing had started after Johnnie, but Jake had managed to spring up and block his way, only to be bludgeoned aside, to fall back in the chair.

'Leave the boy, Cole!' Carmen de Menendez roared. 'Cover them!'

And with a vicious punch she caught Elly on the temple. Instantly, Elly crumpled to the ground in a daze.

'OK, that's enough,' the saloon owner cried, ratcheting back the hammer of her gun. She pointed at Yucatan. 'Don't just sit there, you fool. Get after him. Kill him!'

Jake Scudder stared in amazement as the large servant slipped the loops of rope off his wrists and charged from the room.

★   ★   ★

Johnnie Parker had wrangled nearly all of his adult life and he bounded onto the nearest animal, which happened to be Trixie, Elly's cow pony. Then he took off at a racing pace.

Yucatan, bigger, more ponderous, yet still skilled with horses, selected Rubal Cage's horse. It was a large, fast animal and before long he was gaining on his quarry. The race did not last long. Yucatan rode alongside then heaved himself from the saddle, snatching Johnnie in a bear-hug, to land in a painful bundle in the sand. They rolled over and over, then Yucatan, far heavier and stronger succeeded in fending off Johnnie's weakened blows to pinion him to the ground with his knees. And then his strong hands were about Johnnie's throat, squeezing the life from him.

'Yucatan! Let him go!'

The big servant looked up slowly to see a young Apache dressed in range clothes and a black Stetson dismount from a big black stallion.

'I have looked for you for many moons, you murdering rapist!'

A slow sneer spread across the big

man's face and he contemptuously left the limp form of Johnnie Parker and stood up.

'So, Nantan wants to meet his sister!' He gave an evil leer. Reaching behind him he drew out a wicked-looking double-edged knife. 'I enjoyed your sister.'

Nantan drew his own hunting knife. 'Prepare to die, Yucatan.'

They both dropped into fighting positions, Nantan adopting a thrusting approach as opposed to Yucatan's backward slashing method. For a few moments they tested each other. Then Yucatan rushed in, fending aside Nantan's thrust as he caught and immobilized his arm against his side, while he raised his own knife to stab Nantan's exposed back.

But Johnnie had rolled and gasped enough air to recover sufficiently to realize that his saviour needed help. He scooped a handful of sand, dived forward and threw it in Yucatan's face.

The huge renegade staggered back,

rubbing frenziedly at his tightly screwed eyes as the irritant sand seared his eyeballs. Then Nantan plunged his knife into Yucatan's black heart.

'That is one vow I have kept,' he said staring into the sun.

12

Jake Scudder shook his head with a humourless smile. 'That all kind of makes sense now,' he said as Elly pushed herself back along the floor to lean against the couch.

Carmen de Menendez nodded approvingly. 'Go on, Jake Scudder. Your intelligence impresses me — for a man!'

'Thank you, ma'am. But maybe we should just ask Saul Horrocks here,' Jake replied, turning to Saul. 'I guess there is no need for you to bother with that fake rope any more, is there?'

A thin smile spread across Saul Horrocks's face and with a shake of the head he slipped the coils of rope off his wrists. 'No Jake, you are right. And there is no need for this little charade any longer, either.' He grabbed the neatly laid blanket over his legs then whipped it aside and heaved himself out of the Bath chair.

'Saul!' Elly gasped. 'You . . . you can walk!'

'Poor Elly,' he replied with mock sympathy. 'Always so gullible, weren't you?' Then his expression changed to one of pure hate. 'You snivelling little bitch! You always were Pa's little angel.'

Elly was shaking her head in disbelief. 'But why, Saul? Why? Were you never really paralysed?'

Saul Horrocks tossed his head back and laughed sarcastically. 'Paralysed? Of course not! That was just a little flesh wound — painful and suitably bloody, I admit — that I got Yucatan to give me after he shot that old bastard.'

'You? You had Pa killed? You . . . you monster!'

Saul blew air scornfully through his lips. 'Yeah, well he was a monster to me all of my life, until he thought I could be of use to him. But by then it was too late. I wanted all he had. That is why I and my darling wife, Carmen here, cooked up this plan with Rubal Cage and Yucatan.'

Jake interrupted. 'So you stole the bank's gold that your pa had just borrowed, and you played the invalid. Then you arranged to steal your own herd.'

'Well, half the herd, as you already know. It was a good cover and made everyone think that I was serious. And as a result of all this we were going to get Elly married off to Jeb Jackson.'

Carmen de Menendez kissed her husband on the cheek. 'After we had taken the ransom he would pay, of course.'

Elly stared in blank horror at her brother and his unknown wife, as if seeing the real Saul for the first time in her life. 'And you seriously thought that I would marry Jeb Jackson — out of gratitude!'

Carmen de Menendez scoffed. 'Of course you would. And with his help, it would get the Rocking H back on its feet with Saul at the helm on his own.

Then after a while Jackson would have a fatal accident — maybe the two of you would — and who do you think would inherit the Double J ranch and all that wealth?' She put an arm about Saul's waist and kissed him again. 'Why it would be your dear brother Saul, of course. And then I would appear and 'marry' Saul — and be where I should be — the señora of the largest hacienda north of the border.'

Saul growled and nodded at the body hanging over the window ledge. 'Except we were surrounded by fools and bunglers. Not the least of them was Rubal Cage. The stupid bastard ruined everything.'

Carmen de Menendez patted his arm. 'Not everything, Saul my dear. It can all still work. When the lawmen find these bodies,' she hesitated a moment, then went on, 'including that of your sister — wearing Jackson's engagement ring.'

Saul Horrocks opened his eyes wide as if he saw bright illumination where there had only been darkness. 'Of course. And it will all be put down to Scudder.'

'That's right,' replied his wife. 'He is a wanted murderer, after all. He slit poor Rosalind's throat back in Silver City.'

Cole Lancing had been watching and enjoying the little tableau being played out in front of him, but at this news he experienced a flash of illumination himself. His mind went back to his conversation with Carmen de Menendez on their journey to the Rocking H the previous night. It was clear to him now. Up until then he knew that Scudder had been framed for something, but he had not realized what. But now, to his horror he realized that Carmen de Menendez had killed Rosalind by cutting her throat.

'You killed Rosalind, you murdering bitch!' he exclaimed, his fear of the saloon-owner now replaced by pure fury.

Carmen de Menendez spun round,

having half-forgotten Cole Lancing's part in the scheme of things. And now a glance at his face told her that she would not be able to smooth things over this time. She made an instant decision and reacted by bringing her gun round. Lancing had to die.

But Cole Lancing had seen red and all subservience towards her was swept aside. In his mind he heard the words she had uttered to him the night before — '*I will take care of you, Cole!*'

He fired, saw the red stain spread out over her heart as she was hurled backwards against the wall.

'S . . . Saul!' she gasped, her gun dropping from her hand as she started to sag. Then Lancing fired again and her body jack-knifed, then slid down, dragging a red streak of blood on the wall as she fell.

Saul Horrocks had stared aghast for a moment, but now went for the gun she had dropped, blind fury and hate written across his face. But Jake was on his feet and delivered a two-handed haymaker that lifted him off his feet to land in an unconscious heap in the Bath chair that had for so long been the symbol of his lies and deceit.

'Now it is your turn, Scudder!' Cole Lancing said, turning towards Jake.

But he was stopped by Elly's warning shout. 'Don't move a muscle, or I will shoot you dead!'

Lancing froze with his gun pointing at Jake. Then slowly he swivelled his head to see Elly Horrocks kneeling on the floor with Carmen de Menendez's gun in her two outstretched hands. He grinned, his lazy eye almost languid, as if he felt no cause for fear from her.

'Do you reckon you could kill a man, lady?' he asked, doubtfully. 'It isn't easy, you know. But if you are going to do it, better do it — '

Suddenly another voice piped up from the door. 'Maybe she won't need to,' said Johnnie Parker, standing at the door with a Winchester primed and aimed at Cole Lancing. 'Now if I am right, you are one of the murdering dogs who killed my friends.'

A dew of perspiration had formed on Lancing's forehead, and he vigorously shook his head. 'I never killed anyone, except in a fair fight.'

'Is that so,' replied Johnnie Parker. 'In that case I am going to give you a chance in a fair fight. Now holster that weapon.'

Lancing stared at him in amazement, and then with a contemptuous smile he did as he was bid.

Jake Scudder shook his head. 'Don't do this, Johnnie. This man deserves a proper trial and a rope.'

'Jake, stay out of this, please,' Johnnie replied. Then to Elly:

'Darling, I am going to strap on Cage's gunbelt. If he moves while I get it — shoot him dead!'

Elly bit her lip. 'OK, Johnnie, but I . . . I think Jake is right.'

But Johnnie had already laid down his Winchester and reached for the buckle of Cage's gunbelt. It was then that Cole Lancing saw his chance. He reckoned that if he could down Johnnie he could then easily take the girl.

His gun had just cleared leather when he felt a thud in his chest. Disbelievingly, he looked down and to his horror saw the handle of a hunting knife protruding from the front of his chest. Blood frothed from his mouth and he began to stagger as blood flowed freely down his front.

They all watched as the rustler's body began to convulse. Then he fell back, his lazy eye for once momentarily moving in harmony with the other until the convulsion ended and his sightless eyes stared ceilingwards.

Johnnie turned and nodded at Nantan. 'That is twice you have saved me, Nantan. Thanks.'

Nantan shook his head. 'We are even, my friend. I would be dead by now if you had not blinded Yucatan.'

The sound of horses outside was followed moments later by the entrance of Constable Matt Brooks and his deputy, Samuel McCaid.

'My God — a bloodbath, and no mistake,' gasped Pebble-eye McCaid.

Matt Brooks advanced towards Jake. 'Nantan told me all about you, Scudder. I guess you will be glad to know that I have the sheriff of Silver City and his posse in custody in Tucksville. He seems mighty keen to have you hanged.'

Elly had rushed to embrace Johnnie as he staggered after all his exertions. She helped him to the couch and then turned to the constable.

'There is only one person in this room who needs a rope, Constable, and it isn't Jake Scudder.' She pointed at her brother, her voice quavering with emotion. 'It is that . . . that thing, that used to be my kin.'

And between them, they explained all about the plot, the massacre and the murder of Jeb Jackson.

'I never did take to that sheriff of Silver City,' Matt Brooks said. 'He certainly is a pitiful excuse for a lawman. Not like my deputy here.'

215

Despite himself, Deputy McCaid blushed. 'We are a team, Constable. We are a team.'

Saul Horrocks looked dazed a few moments later as he came round, to find the myopic deputy of Tucksville locking manacles on his wrists.

* * *

A week later Johnnie Parker and Elly Horrocks were married in Tucksville, a week before the trial of her brother Saul Horrocks.

'We wanted that monster to see that despite all of his murdering and deviousness, we were man and wife,' Elly explained to Jake and Nantan.

'It will be hard,' Johnnie said. 'Saul Horrocks was rotten to the core, but he is still her natural born brother, so she is bound to be torn up about it all — especially when he is sentenced to be hanged, which he surely will be.'

They ate a quiet supper together, then the following morning Jake and

TROUBLE AT BRODIE CREEK

Ben Coady

Sam Hanley, marshal of Brodie Creek, has resigned to marry and become a rancher. However, trouble hits town when the Thad Cross gang — all killers — arrive. To avert disaster the townsfolk want Hanley back as marshal, but Hanley only becomes involved when the Cross gang raid the bank and kidnap his new wife, Ellie. To rescue Ellie he must follow Cross to Hangman's Perch, an impregnable outlaw roost. Everything seems stacked against him — can Hanley win through?

WHERE ONE MAN STANDS

Chad Hammer

The brothers had never been close —until a killer cut down their father at the end of the long trail drive. That was the day their world would change forever. Side by side they set out to battle the killer they hunted and the murderous desert. Until that day and hour when they faced their man, not as enemies but as true brothers with but a single thought. Revenge or death! They would accept nothing less — together.

SIDEWINDER FLATS

Walt Masterton

When horse trader Con Carnigan's cavalry horses are stolen, he faces starvation if he cannot retrieve them. He tracks them to Sidewinder Flats in the Sonoran Desert, but finds himself in the domain of a western Fagin. The town is a robbers' roost run by Hoffman, who offers Carnigan the sheriff's job, so long as he turns a blind eye to the criminals. Carnigan however, takes the job seriously, as Hoffman and his cohorts discover . . .

A PLACE CALLED JEOPARDY

Eugene Clifton

Sheriff Matt Turner's authority is usurped when Duke Coulter arrives in Jeopardy. Coulter is an ambitious, but unscrupulous man with a handful of hired guns. Townsfolk are dying and Matt finds himself powerless to do anything about it, as a man called Logan now wears the sheriff's badge, and Matt, with a price on his head, must run for his life. To bring justice back to Jeopardy, he'll have to fight on the other side of the law.

WARRICK'S BATTLE

Terrell L. Bowers

Haunted by the past, Paul Warrick is assailed by bad memories, and in an attempt to forget, drifts from town to town finding work. But a shoot-out at a casino lands him in jail, and with the valley on the verge of a range war, Paul's actions might be the fire to light the fuse. Paul becomes involved in the final showdown — and he must not only save his life, but also his own sanity at the same time!

MAN OF BLOOD

Lee Lejeune

When he visits his brother, Texas Ranger Tom Flint finds Hank dying and his wife Abby abducted after an attack on their homestead. Soon Flint runs up against a gang of vicious layabouts working for Rodney Ravenshaw, who is trying to retrieve family property by underhand means. Can Flint live up to his Comanche name of Man of Blood and save his brother's homestead by ridding the town of Willow Creek of its nest of vipers?

Nantan rode off together. Neither of them had any place in particular to go, and neither knew how long they would ride together. For now there was just one trail that they meant to follow. That was the one leading away from so much tragedy and so much death. It was the trail that passed through Rattlesnake Pass.

THE END